Al Cody

THE RANCH AT POWDER RIVER

G.K.HALL&CO.
Boston, Massachusetts
1990

Published in Large Print by arrangement with
Bobbe Siegel Literary Agency.

G.K. Hall Large Print Book Series.

Set in 16 pt. Plantin.

Library of Congress Cataloging in Publication Data

Cody, Al , 1899–.
The Ranch at Powder River / Al Cody.
p. cm—(G.K. Hall large print book series) (Nightingale series)
ISBN 0-8161-4958-5 (lg. print)
1. Large type books. I. Title.
[PS3519.O712R3 1990]
813'.54—dc20 89-26796

I

The sun cast slanting long rays across a rough and broken land, but the sharp chill of dawn clung to the air. Off to the south, breaks in the hills afforded Montana Abbott occasional glimpses of the Yellowstone, running as turgid as its name. The water and the cottonwoods which lined its course were partly obscured by rising mists from the river, looking curiously like puffs of gunsmoke. As if to add to the reality of the illusion, a gun growled throatily from considerably closer at hand.

The big bay cayuse on which Montana was mounted snorted its dislike, jerking its ugly hammerhead. The horse seemed to have as deep an aversion to guns as he did, and Montana had long since learned that their booming was usually a portent of trouble.

The gun rasped again, followed by a sharper, even more chilling sound—a keening, high-pitched wailing, once heard never to be forgotten. It reminded him of a werewolf's cry, the war whoops of Indians on the attack.

The long leanness of his big body went tense, as much from surprise as the ever-recurring emotion which came with the threat of danger. This thumbscrewing of the nerves was not exactly fear, and no man had ever questioned his courage. But after a dozen battles and a score of lesser skirmishes, it was always the same: a dryness of the mouth, tightness which squeezed like a bull-dog's jaws, the prickling of apprehension. Like the river mists in the sun, such tensions evaporated when threat became action, but he had long since realized that he'd never outgrow the initial chilling impact.

The big hammerhead paused at the sound, while a shiver worked up from its hoofs as though it, too, had heard such sounds before. Nightmare noises went ill with the morning sun.

Also, technically at least, there was a truce if not peace between red men and white. This absence of active animosity was of recent origin, but like a worn rope, quick to fray. Young bucks had to prove their manhood, riding adventurously, satisfying ancient cravings. Such rovers found temptation hard to resist when they came upon a few straggling white men who offered the promise of easy scalps.

"Reckon we'd better have a look," Montana told the horse, and the hammerhead, obedient to a pressure of knees and reins, swung as he directed. Which was probably a foolish thing to do, and might well prove foolhardy, since he could as easily have kept going, closing his ears to sounds of strife and despair. But in so lonesome a country, and with fellow-men in such a fix, a man did what he could.

Once more, in the next few minutes, the gun growled its defiance, but the long spaces between shots bespoke desperation and perhaps a shortage of ammunition. Here the hills peaked a couple of miles back from the river, long and half-naked ridges like loaves of bread baking in the sun, their timber cover of evergreens scanty and remote. If any of these trees had echoed to birdsong at the approach of the sun, such lilting had hushed in dread before the harsher assaults.

The big cayuse climbed a final slope, hoof-falls muted by the grassy carpet, then halted at a touch. Twin bowls were spread out below. The nearer was directly ahead, a rock-walled enclosure of no great size, less than a hundred feet across. As though nature had envisioned what was now taking place and prepared an amphitheatre, the first bowl provided an excellent fortress, overlooking the larger bowl, considerably farther down the hill.

Leaving his horse on the sheltered side of the crest, Montana made use of the lookout, assessing the situation.

The view was reasonably good, and what it disclosed was not too different from what he had expected. The larger bowl, below, was nearly a quarter of a mile in width, sufficiently broken and boulder-studded to afford some shelter both for fugitives and attackers. He made out a couple of the besieged near the middle of the enclosure, crouched amid a tangle of stones. The ripple of the early sun along a gun barrel served as a focus.

A couple of horses stood nervously in a partly sheltered screen of brush, not far to the side. He had the picture. The two had been surprised. Forted up, they were besieged.

It took another couple of minutes, studying the bowl above as well as the one below them, to decide that at least half a dozen warriors were spread around it, occasionally loosing an arrow, endeavoring to slip from one covering boulder to another, closing the ring. Not much was actually to be seen, but enough to give him the picture.

Both groups had fallen silent, growing more deadly as the climax neared. The stones which afforded cover also made it easy for the attackers to creep in. If any help was to be given, it would have to be soon.

There was the rub. Even should he take a hand, the odds would remain heavy, almost overwhelming. The end result could well be not the saving of the threatened scalps of the besieged pair, but the addition of his own to the collection.

The warriors blended well with the terrain and were difficult to locate. Perhaps deceived by the hush, a magpie came winging, to veer abruptly and increase the beat of its wings. Guided by what it had seen, Montana made out part of a bared brown back, a half-shaven head adorned with a single feather. It was good enough as a target, but too far off for him to be sure whether the brave was Blackfoot or Sioux, Crow or a wanderer from some more distant tribe. Not that it made a great deal of difference. A tame house cat never lost its lust for mice or birds, and the comparison extended to this case.

He sensed a restlessness, a stirring as though the attackers were about ready to chance a rush, a finish marked by overwhelming power. He might delay if not avert that with a few well-placed bullets, but as a former captain of cavalry, he preferred a battle plan which afforded at least a chance for victory.

Surprise would favor him. If he could build upon that—

Montana worked swiftly. The six-shooter in his holster he set in position beside an upthrusting finger of stone, tying it with a short length of fish line. Always, as a matter of prudence, he carried a coil of such cord, along with hooks. Together they had provided many a meal of trout, and it had been in his mind to cut a willow for a rod and whip some small stream for his breakfast, when the fight sounds had interrupted.

A slip knot at the end of the line curved around the trigger. Drawing back the hammer of the Colt's to full cock, he moved across to the far side of the small bowl, playing out the fish line as he moved. At the halfway point of the natural wall, a round boulder, as thick as his body, suggested a plan. It was already upon the rocky shelf, and required only a little adjustment to be poised so lightly that a nudge would set it rolling and bounding downslope.

Here was the mix for a devil's broth. Having at times been forced to sup such a brew, Montana found it more palatable when he was the cook. From the far rim of his own bowl, he selected a target, thrusting the snout of his rifle into position. He curled a finger around the trigger, and the instantly responding yell, mingling pain and consternation, accompanied by a wild scrambling, attested to the fact that the shot had not been wasted.

Promptly, from another point, the revolver boomed as he jerked the trip line. He fired the rifle again, as surprise startled another warrior to make an incautious move, then snatched a stone the size of his fist. His aim was good, and the impact of the missile against the delicately balanced boulder worked precisely as he had hoped. It went tumbling, crashing and bounding in a noisy frenzy all out of proportion to what damage it might wreak.

A third shot from the rifle was followed moments later by another from the Colt's, as he reached and snatched it up. A couple of extra bullets served as good measure but were otherwise wasted, since by then the demoralized besiegers were in full retreat, already out of sight and range. They fled with the certainty that not only the tables were turned, but that a sizable rescue party was above.

Recoiling his fish line and reloading his weapons, Montana descended to the larger bowl, leading his horse. That the two men had been in dire straits was immediately apparent. One lay outstretched in a pool of his own blood, an arrow protruding from both chest and back. He was unconscious, if not already dead.

His companion was in better shape, but not much, from the standpoint of effective resistance. Another arrow had gashed his right arm below the elbow, a bloody if not otherwise ugly wound, but bad enough pretty well to spoil his marksmanship. A reddish stubble of whiskers, the grime and dishevelment of battle, disguised but could not conceal the marks of an old soldier. He eyed Montana with surprise, incredulity and gratification.

"I'm pleased to see you, stranger," he observed. "Which same goes for Bill Jameson here, even if he can't speak for himself. But you didn't create all that unholy ruckus by your own self, did you now?"

"Such as it was," Montana acknowledged. "A diversion seemed to be called for."

"It sure was. Them red devils jumped us without no warnin'—risin' just like the sun. They was just nervin' themselves to come on in and finish us off—which they could have done, easy enough. Is he—dead?"

Montana was examining Jameson. Of medium build, he was wiry, muscled like a cougar, with thinning hair of a cougar's pale tawniness. Montana's head shake was grim at thought of the chore yet to be done.

"Not yet, at least. But this arrow has got to come out. Which operation he may or may not survive."

In preparation, he stripped off his own shirt, tearing it into long strips. Mercifully, the wounded man remained unconscious. But a groan was twisted from white lips as Montana took the protruding barb of the arrow in both hands and broke it with a swift motion, then, seizing the haft on the opposite side, pulled swiftly and strongly to extricate the crimson rod. Its removal was followed by twin gusts of blood.

Moss grew on the side of one of the boulders where the fugitives had sheltered. He used chunks of it to cover the arrow punctures, bandaging the wounds as well as possible with the strips of cloth. Presently, when the bleeding was reasonably well checked, he made sure, with some surprise, that the injured man was still breathing.

Inquiry widened the eyes of his companion.

"Has he got a chance?"

Montana was tempted to make an admission of the stark truth. Under the best of conditions and care, the wound was ugly, and survival would be uncertain, the odds against it high. Lacking such care and the skill of a doctor, there was even less possibility.

"Sure'd hate to see the cap'n go under now, in such fashion," the other man went on, his words confirming the impression which Montana had already received. These two had been soldiers, the one probably a sergeant. The stamp of the army was as indelible on a man's character as the loyalty which non-coms sometimes felt for the commanders with whom they had served across years of strife. "Folks used to call him Old Indestructible. And for a measly arrow to do him in—"

"You never can tell," Montana said. "We'd better get going, see if we can find help."

The old sergeant's gaze was bleak with comprehension.

"And the chances of that, hereabouts, ain't half as good as stagin' a snowball fight in Hades." He nodded. "But still, *you* turned up in the nick of time—"

On his own horse again, cradling Captain Jameson in front of the saddle, Montana swung toward the river. If any hope existed, it would be along the watercourse. Not that his expectations were any higher than those which the sergeant had voiced.

Then, from near the crest of the line of bluffs, with the river a gleam of silver in the sun, he stared, shook his head and marveled. Old Indestructible! Perhaps there was something in the name, after all.

So far away as to give the appearance of a bird on a pond, a river packet was breasting the current of the Yellowstone. River boats were increasingly common on the Missouri, but they rarely ventured onto the dangerously taboo waters of the forbidden Yellowstone. By tacit, sometimes even formal agreement between the angry red men and the Great White Father, the territory abutting the flowing yellow waters was reserved for the red men and forbidden to the white.

Not that all white men obeyed governmental injunctions or were impressed by threats.

A river packet here, under such circumstances, seemed in the nature of a miracle. Montana was of no mind to question or argue. There might even be a doctor aboard the boat. If they could signal her and get the wounded man on board, then he would have discharged his responsibility.

II

The gentleman who promenaded the available deck spaces of the river packet Star of the West preferred to be known as the Right Honorable Henry Tiller-Parsons. Clad elegantly if inappropriately in spats, he gazed about with the air of a monarch surveying his domain. Perhaps rightly, for what he had done during recent weeks certainly could have been rated as an accomplishment, the crowded condition of the packet furnishing additional proof of what had been or was still to be.

Practically the entire capacity of the sternwheeler, whose captain boasted that she could run, if necessary, on a heavy dew, was given over to a variety of freight. Its ultimate destination was tagged or lettered as the Powder River Ranch. Stacks of lumber, boxes of tools, cartons of hardware were piled under and around a sleek-looking buggy. A pair of heavy wagons had their double boxes already loaded with staple groceries. Household furniture vied with other items of a surprising nature. All of this was being brought as far as the mouth of the Powder River at Tiller-Parsons' direction.

Removing a glove, he gave a complacent twist to a small, neatly waxed mustache, watching the slow alteration of the landscape as they churned against the current. To attain his present position had taken some little while, together with a mixture of servility to his betters on the one hand, and effrontery to all others whom he could afford to bully; there had been as much luck as ability, almost as many downs as ups, but he was finally reaching the goals which he had set for himself. The Star and what it carried was proof.

Most of the merchandise had been loaded at St. Louis. For one man to charter a river boat for the long passage up the Missouri was unheard of and had excited comment. He had made the commitments and paid necessary bills in the name of the Powder River Ranch Company, as its manager. Sums, little short of staggering even to himself, had passed through his hands. But such expenditures had been necessary. Money spoke with a convincing voice, especially where Captain Ira Shaumut was concerned.

"You must have good backing for this ranch," Shaumut had observed. "A syndicate, I take it?"

"A syndicate of English gentlemen," Tiller-Parsons confirmed. "Sir John Crispin is one of the directors." He added with easy complacence, "By another spring, the Powder River Ranch should be the largest operation of its type in the territory of Montana. Our ranch headquarters are back in the hills, half a hundred miles from the Yellowstone. A house is already in the process of erection, but some of these supplies will be used to finish and furnish it."

"A house, did you say?" Shaumut gibed. "Wouldn't a mansion be closer to the fact?"

Tiller-Parsons preened his mustache, his somewhat prominent eyes goggling.

"There will be some resemblances, certainly," he confirmed. "While I will occupy it as manager, the real purpose is to provide adequate accommodations for the owners, when they may see fit to visit the ranch. For that, something along the lines of an English country estate is called for. I would not want to disappoint them."

"Naturally not," Shaumut agreed, regarding Tiller-Parsons with a grudging respect. Something about the man was not quite right; there was some quality which grated, for all the superficial smoothness which he exuded. But if he possessed the trust of his employers and had the ability to manage a ranch of such proportions, there must be more to him than met the eye.

Fort Benton had been the original destination of the Star of the West, but the charter and full consignment of cargo had persuaded Shaumut to turn into the little known waters of the Yellowstone and proceed as far as the mouth of the Powder, a stream which in appearance he found far less impressive than its name. Having made fast near the shore, they proceeded with the business of unloading, under the watchful and somewhat nervous eye of Tiller-Parsons.

Setting foot on solid ground again, this apprehension he carefully concealed, along with the immediate reason for the apprehension. In fact, he took pains to hide it under a stream of light and airy conversation with the lady herself. Miss Alicia Fredericks had proved a charming companion during the long miles up from St. Louis.

Her original destination, booked prior to the chartering, like that of most of the other passengers, had been Fort Benton rather than Powder River. But when the matter of the freight had been explained, along with the need for haste in delivering it, Tiller-Parsons had proved convincing. Captain Shaumut had offered to return any fares paid in advance, or to secure the passengers accommodations aboard another river packet. But Tiller-Parsons, with an eye to the considerable sums involved, had suggested that the Star first proceed up the Yellowstone, then return to the Missouri and so on to Benton, affording everyone several extra days of voyaging and scenery at no extra cost. To that there had been general agreement, the others following where Alicia led.

That they should do so was not surprising. Not only was she an extremely goodlooking woman, of an adventuresome disposition, as taking such a trip, attended only by a maid, attested; in her native New Orleans she was an arbiter of fashion and society. That sprang partly from her own good looks and accomplishments, in part from the wealth belonging to the Fredericks.

Hearing the proportions of that wealth, Tiller-Parsons had been as dazzled by the possibilities as by the lady. At the outset he had hesitated, though briefly, uncertain what course he should take, weighing the rewards against the risks. An easy compromise had been to accommodate the original list of passengers.

By the third day out from St. Louis, he had made his decision, encouraged by the graciousness with which Alicia Fredericks accepted him as an equal, or perhaps as a suitor. Complacently, he had given an added twist to his mustache, surveying himself in the mirror of his room. Men might, in fact often did dislike him, but with the ladies it was a different story. He was where he was today by reason of his ability to charm the fair sex.

One example had been Sir John Crispin's lady. She had swung a close balance in his favor, approving him to manage the big ranch for the syndicate, persuading her husband to influence the other stockholders. And she was but one of several bedazzled ladies.

That the effect had a way of wearing off,

on longer acquaintance, Tiller-Parsons had discovered to be an asset rather than a liability. The process enabled him, on general principles, to love them and leave them, which was also profitable.

Now, though giving no outward sign, he found himself on the long horns of a dilemma. The considerable load of supplies had to be transported to the ranch headquarters, and the work pushed with all possible speed. The house had to be enclosed before the advent of bad weather, and enough accomplished along other lines to confirm Sir John's judgment and reassure the others that he was the proper man to manage the enterprise. Failure could bring an unwelcome probing into the lavish manner in which he had been spending the assets of the syndicate.

He should go along with the loads of freight, supervising the work. Just as imperatively, he must go back down-river on the Star, continuing to dance attendance on Alicia Fredericks. Such an easy gesture on his part, signifying affluence along with a careless ability to manage everything, would, he was certain, accomplish the desired result: to wit, to stand before a parson, perhaps at Fort Benton, with Alicia by his side.

The immediate difficulty was that by taking such a course he might lose his position as manager of the syndicate, which at this particular juncture would be highly undesirable. But to get his hands on the Fredericks wealth was at least equally tempting.

There should be a way to do both. But his mind, usually agile, was slow in coming up with a solution.

Hopefully he noted a pair of new arrivals and, excusing himself, hurried to meet them. One he recognized as a cowboy already in his employ at the ranch. The other he took for a second hand. He had left instructions that his ranch foreman should be at the Powder on or before this date, to await the arrival of the chartered craft. Anxiously he confirmed that there was no sign of the foreman.

Timothy O'Donnell, ex-sergeant of cavalry, C. S. A., was bluff and hearty, not to say capable. He gave Tiller-Parsons the bad news in one stiff swallow.

"Jones wa'n't able to come. He's dead."

"Dead?" Tiller-Parsons echoed, and swallowed painfully. He had almost persuaded himself that it might be safe to entrust everything to Jones, in addition to the work with the cattle. Jones was only a cowboy, but he was a man who knew cattle—and so essential, since Tiller-Parsons did not. But when that had been said, all the facts were encompassed. Jones was—or had been—a cowboy. That was all.

O'Donnell nodded, his face carefully blank. "He got the herd you wanted up from Texas. But there was a smidgin of trouble, a gun battle. We had to bury him."

Tiller-Parsons digested this news, carefully asking no questions. It was a relief that the herd had been delivered, even if Jones had lost his life in the operation. Tiller-Parsons' long-range plans, like those of his employers, were centered in a big beef herd, and he had made promises which might have fallen short.

So that part of the report was a relief. But it was highly inconvenient that the foreman had gotten himself killed at this particular time.

From being a lonely spot in a wide land, this mouth of the Powder was suddenly becoming populous. Another contingent of riders was coming up, and Tiller-Parsons, always observant and sharp of wit as necessity demanded, noted that one man held another, who appeared to be either sick or wounded, on the front of his saddle.

During the next several minutes, as Montana Abbott made the welcome discovery that there was a doctor on board the packet, then carried Bill Jameson and delivered him into the doctor's care, Tiller-Parsons learned in his turn that this man was Montana Abbott. Though his wispy mustache was his closest physical resemblance to a fox, Tiller-Parsons' ears figuratively perked up at the news.

Presently he found an opportunity to introduce himself, extending his hand.

"I've heard of you, Abbott," he said. "It's a pleasure to know you, sir."

Montana accepted the handshake without particular enthusiasm. Ladies might find Tiller-Parsons attractive. He did not.

Tiller-Parsons went on to explain himself, also the considerable amount of freight which was still being unloaded. He had already come to a decision.

"The Indian attack of which you speak, and its consequences, was certainly regrettable, but the end result of it, which was to bring you here at this particular time, I find most opportune," he said smoothly. "Except for the business of the Powder River Ranch and this cargo, the Star of the West would not have arrived at this particular place in

Mr. Jameson's hour of need. Nor would you in *my* time of need."

Montana's eyebrows lifted in faint inquiry.

"I've just received bad news," Tiller-Parsons explained. "My ranch foreman was killed in a gunfight with cattle rustlers. His loss, especially at this particular time, puts me in a bad fix. Not every man—in fact, very few—is capable of doing what has to be done."

That, judging by the scope of operations suggested by the mountain of freight, was perhaps true. Montana waited politely.

"I've heard of you—favorably," Tiller-Parsons went on, with only faint condescension. "You are an experienced cattleman, and as a former army officer, also experienced in leadership; in short, the sort of man I require. I hope I find you at loose ends, sir. I'd like to hire you as foreman of the Powder River Ranch."

Montana was incredulous. He had not expected anything of the sort.

Such a position might be quite a job—and he could use a job. On the other hand, he could feel no enthusiasm at the prospect of working for Tiller-Parsons. His prejudice might be irrational, but it had been formed. He didn't like the man.

"I have to return down-river with the boat, then up to Fort Benton, after which I will journey to the ranch," Tiller-Parsons went on. "As foreman, you will be in charge of all operations during my absence, not only as regards the cattle and the running of the ranch, but also when it comes to seeing that the buildings are properly erected with the least possible delay."

"But you don't know a thing about me, or whether I could handle such a job," Montana protested.

"On the contrary, I've heard quite a lot about you, Mr. Abbott—and I flatter myself that I am a judge of character. The job is yours if you will take it." He played his trump card.

"Your salary will be two thousand dollars a year, plus board and quarters, starting as of now."

Montana drew a deep breath. He'd intended to say no—but this sounded challenging as well as interesting. And the pay was far above what he would be able to command as a cowhand.

"You've hired yourself a man," he said.

III

Tiller-Parsons was elated. There was no doubt in his mind that Abbott was a good man, who would be able to handle affairs at the ranch during his absence, and that was fine for the immediate present. But it was the long view which chiefly concerned him, the carrying out of plans which had been set in motion a long while before. The killing of Jones had posed a threat, but by this gesture he had pretty well retrieved the situation.

Montana Abbott was well known beyond the Territory as an honest man of unimpeachable integrity. Such a reputation was precisely what Tiller-Parsons required at the moment.

A measure of his pleasure showed through as he introduced Montana to Alicia Fredericks. He displayed a ponderous playfulness akin to that of a dancing elephant.

"My dear, this is Montana Abbott, of whom you may have heard. He has quite a reputation for getting things done, and I'm particularly fortunate in having him take charge at the ranch so that I can devote myself to other matters of equal or even greater importance—affairs such as roses and moonlight."

His meaning could hardly be misunderstood, as Alicia showed by blushing in emulation of the rose. Clearly she was not displeased. Montana shrugged and put it from his mind. It was none of his business, though he found it somewhat incomprehensible. He had wondered more than once why the most lovely women seemed to be attracted by worthless men—though in view of his position, perhaps that was unjust as applied to Tiller-Parsons.

The physician on board the Star of the West was taking such care as was possible of Captain Bill Jameson, and perhaps his reputation as Old Indestructible, along with the doctor's skill, would carry him through. In any case, there was nothing more that Montana could do for him, and the series of events had led to his acquiring an unlooked-for job at a very good salary.

Tiller-Parsons filled him in on the general situation, giving some last-minute instructions, along with funds for expenses. Then the Star of the West backed to midstream and began the return trip to the Missouri. Timothy O'Donnell was displaying the qualities of a sergeant, getting the freight loaded onto the wagons, with the excess stored for a later date, as they made ready to head for the ranch.

"It's an amazin' set-up," he confided to Montana. "Them crazy Englishmen must be made of money, judgin' by the way Tiller-Parsons has been throwin' it around. Likely they've heard of lots of land and big herds in this country, and figure that it adds up to a deal where they can't help but make fortunes. Cows have calves, they eat grass and grow up, your herd gets bigger and bigger!" He grinned sardonically. "Of course it could work out that way, but I'd want somebody else managin' the job, if it was me."

Montana volunteered no comment, although the opinion jibed with his own. Undeterred, O'Donnell went on:

"Tiller-Parsons! What sort of a name is that? Sounds like a horse's snort. Sure he's the boss, and I'm takin' some of the money he's throwin' around, and I'll do my best to earn it. But all I've got to say is, I figure those Englishmen have got a lot to learn."

While that might be true, it should be interesting to work for a syndicate whose notion of a cattle ranch was perhaps entangled with ideas of English country estates and hunting expeditions along the frontier.

By nightfall, the laden wagons had left the river well behind. The next day's journey was uneventful, the slow miles unrolling along a wide and empty land. Besides himself and O'Donnell, there were eight other men to handle the teams and wagons. They halted short of sunset, and the cook soon had a tempting collection of aromas rising, much as the mists had risen above the water. His grin was a little awed.

"I've been kind of pokin' into the supplies we unloaded yesterday, and samplin' some things that I've heard of but never come across before," he explained. "I ain't never seen the like of it, not for grub. We'll eat like a hog in a 'tater patch."

Hunkered back from the fire glow, with a tin plate and a coffee cup, Montana agreed. For one thing, this was real coffee, ordinarily diffcult to obtain. A well-cured ham was easily the best that he'd tasted since before the war.

Something stirred among the brush at the rear. Montana turned swiftly, gun in hand, then lowered it uncertainly at a startled gasp. His own reaction was one of equal surprise. Whatever he had expected, it had not been a woman, her eyes rounding at sight of the gun.

Not only was she a woman, but by no stretch of the imagination could she be classed as ordinary, or belonging to the country thereabouts. She was a shade above normal height, dark hair accenting the fairness of her skin, and a wistful quality of eyes and mouth adding an elusive charm. She might be twenty, possibly a year or so older.

Her face had paled. "I'm sorry," Montana said quickly. "You surprised me—but I didn't mean to startle you."

Tim O'Donnell, on the opposite side of the fire, was staring as though beholding an angel.

"It's all right," the girl said reassuringly as Montana holstered the revolver, and her poise was complemented by graciousness. "You have reason to be alert, to be suspicious, with outlaws close at hand—dangerous ones."

Such words might be a warning, or they could serve as a distraction. Long-standing familiarity with risk had taught him to regard everything with the same suspicion as a fox circling a trap. A partial answer came with unwelcome promptness. From the closing darkness, off in the sunset's last glow, there was a commotion, shouts and snorts and the pounding of hoofs. Their horses were there, mostly the work animals, unharnessed and left to roll and graze before being herded closer for the night.

Even as the girl spoke, raiders were attempting to stampede the horses, to strand them on foot. Not having expected anything of the sort, he had been caught napping. With a remuda of riding ponies such as accompanied a trail herd, such an attempt might be logical. But that anyone might attempt to steal heavy work animals had not entered his mind.

Whatever the object, the raid could be crippling if successful. Already, judging by the sounds, the horses were being put to flight. Overtaking them, much less recovering them, might be difficult.

His own horse, still saddled, was grazing close at hand, dragging the bridle reins. Montana had come late to supper, intending to bunch the others before it grew too dark. Now the girl was speaking again, this time to O'Donnell.

"Here, take my horse," she offered. It had been hidden by the brush and dusk as she dismounted, but she still clung to the reins. Tim O'Donnell nodded, but wasted no time in words. He was up as quickly as Montana; then they spurred in pursuit.

"What a woman!" O'Donnell breathed. "Here, take my horse—just as I'm needin' one, and never a waste of time questionin' and answerin'. It's like she was an angel, droppin' in on us from nowhere!"

Montana was willing to accept his opinion, but his mind was on the business at hand. He urged his cayuse to a burst of speed, glimpsing a flowing huddle of movement ahead, the running animals like spilled ink in the lighter gloom. The shouts of the raiders, as they sought to push the plunging horses to greater speed, suggested perhaps half a dozen men. Initially, favored by surprise, they had succeeded, but the heavy draft animals ran lumberingly, and the swiftness of the pursuit was disconcerting. They had probably hoped to get away with every horse, leaving the men on foot. After that, all the advantage would be with them.

Odds of three to one could be touchy, though in the gloom they did not matter so much. The gap was swiftly closing. Sensing that, the raiders closed ranks, swinging to face their pursuers; then flames stabbed the night like spiteful fireflies. The crack of guns was succeeded by the whistle of a bullet.

The closeness was probably more the result of chance than of a sure aim, and Montana paid no attention, returning the fire. The raiders were shooting in panic, and that was a mistake. Their gun flashes provided targets at which to shoot back.

Like himself, Timothy O'Donnell was demonstrating that he was an old hand at forays of this nature. He knew how to pick a target and make his shots count. Or it might be that, inspired by the sight of an angel, he was outdoing himself.

Their fire was proving uncomfortably accurate, almost devastating. The others continued to blaze away frantically; then panic had its way. One man screamed wildly that he was killed. The loudness of his protestation left some doubt regarding the assertion, but it had its effect on his companions. The sudden neigh of a horse was high with terror. With a common impulse, those who were able to flee did so, swinging, riding with no thought beyond escape.

Their numbers apparently included the

man who had thought himself killed, for only one darker huddle remained as they were swallowed by the night. The blotch against the earth was a downed cayuse, an error which Montana disliked. But in the heat of battle, with poor visibility, mistakes had a way of occurring.

The stampeded work animals, already tired from a long day in the harness, finding themselves no longer driven, were coming to a halt. Montana dismounted beside the downed horse, O'Donnell coming to stand beside him.

A dragging sigh of pain and weariness testified that the rider was still alive, but perhaps not much more than that. A closer look showed the correctness of such a guess. He lay, caught and pinned by the dead horse he had been riding, and the grayness already spreading over his face confirmed Montana's initial opinion that freeing him from the weight would be largely a wasted gesture.

But O'Donnell, not waiting for instructions, was removing a coiled lariat from the saddle which he had borrowed, attaching one end to the nearest hoof of the sprawled cayuse and the other to the saddle-horn. Mounting, he applied leverage, tipping the dead animal over so that the trapped man was freed. Montana knelt beside him.

The injured man's eyes opened as the crushing weight was removed. Pain-washed, they gazed vacantly. The light grew better as the moon, nearly at the full, rolled into sight over the horizon, in the manner of a gopher pushing a mound of dirt from its hole.

The vacancy of the stare gave way to a sort of recognition; the weary eyes focused. To Montana's amazement, there was both resignation and a sharp scorn on his face.

"You made a good shot," he observed. His mind seemed clear, though the tone was hardly above a whisper.

"The luck of the game," Montana agreed. "It might have been the other way."

"Not my luck, mister. It don't run that way—never did. Guess I've got it coming though we had figured to fool you."

"You almost did."

"Almost's not good enough." The bitter scorn seemed as much for himself as for Montana. It welled up in searing laughter, and with that he choked, and a foam of blood appeared on his lips. But presently he controlled himself.

"Likely you're wondering why. But why

not? Why not steal from you blasted thieves? It makes us plain rustlers—but you syndicate skunks ain't lily white."

He seemed impelled to talk, to explain if not to excuse his actions. Montana opened his mouth to caution him, then left the words unsaid. This fellow had very little time to talk left, and further words would not make any particular difference.

"Yeah, we're cattle thieves, all right—tryin' to steal that big herd, and we sure enough botched that, too." Montana supposed that he was referring to the attempt on the trail herd from Texas, the one in which Jones had been killed. Then the dying man's words drew his startled attention.

"Why is it any worse for us to steal the herd from you fellows than for you to rustle those critters from their owners in the first place? Or did you figure nobody'd find out about that massacre down in the Wind River Country?"

His mocking voice stopped. The eyes were still staring up, wide, but no longer angry or sardonic. Montana got slowly to his feet, looking questioningly at O'Donnell, who had overheard. The ex-sergeant slowly shook his head.

"I wouldn't know, Cap'n Abbott," he

said, and his voice as he articulated the title held respect. "A crew delivered the trail herd that we'd been expectin' to the ranch. And as far as I know, the papers on them were in order. But I suppose they could have been rustled somewhere along the trail up from Texas."

Montana considered the matter with a bleak distaste. He'd taken the job as foreman, and that entailed a certain loyalty to the outfit as well as responsibility, but he did not like any of these implications, although the dead man's last words helped explain certain recent events, including the try at stealing the horses.

His assumption that the theft and massacre had been at the orders, or at least with the connivance, of the syndicate might or might not be true. Jones, who had been the man in charge, was dead. Tiller-Parsons was the agent for the syndicate, made up of supposedly honorable men, who were certainly too far away, too strange to this land and its customs, to have much inkling of what was going on.

Nor had Tiller-Parsons been on the ranch or in its vicinity at the time. And that, too, might or might not be pertinent.

O'Donnell helped load the dead man onto

Montana's horse. It snorted and sidled, not liking the burden, the smell of blood making it nervous. But the fellow deserved a decent burial before they went on, at least for his cynical honesty if not for his revelations. Montana led the horse back to camp, and O'Donnell brought in the horse herd.

The night was soft with the hush of summer, the moon lending a mellow quality sharply in contrast to the strife it had witnessed. Montana's thoughts reverted to the woman, who had appeared so strangely, immediately voicing a warning, then lending her horse to O'Donnell. Except for that extra animal in addition to his own, they would probably have been stranded, vulnerable to ambushment and bushwhack.

Who was she, and where had she come from? For any woman, especially any white woman, to materialize in such fashion and at such a time was a reason for surprise. And for a woman apparently of the quality of Alicia Fredericks to come riding into their camp was doubly bewildering.

But probably she could explain herself; he was certainly curious. Brighter crimson flared like a beacon where the dying cook fire had been restored. The rest of the crew were alert and uneasy, awaiting their return.

The girl stood near the fire, finishing the supper with which she had been provided.

Tim O'Donnell reached the camp ahead of Montana. He came leading her horse, sweeping off his hat.

"Here's your horse back," he said. "And many thanks for the loan, ma'am. I don't know whether Montana could have managed that rustlin' crew entirely by himself, good as he is at such chores."

The woman gave O'Donnell a quick smile, but her regard was for Montana as he came up and halted, waiting at the rim of the fire glow. Her eyes were appraising, judging.

"You are more than welcome," she informed O'Donnell, then swung toward Montana. Her voice held a pleasant muted quality. "You are wondering, of course, who I am, where I came from, and why I am here."

Montana did not dissemble. "I guess we are all of us a bit curious, ma'am," he conceded.

"And naturally so. I had heard that your group would be on the way to the ranch with supplies. So it seemed reasonable and proper, under the circumstances, for me to try and join you. I am Rose Tiller-Parsons—Mrs. Tiller-Parsons."

IV

O'Donnell, listening eagerly, overheard. He stared blankly, a comical look of dismay spreading slowly over his face. Montana was equally startled. The woman's assertion that she was Mrs. Tiller-Parsons was at least as surprising as her sudden appearance.

Rose seemed fitting as a name, but Tiller-Parsons did not. Seeing their bewilderment, she explained in more detail.

"My husband has been busy, what with buying supplies and looking after a great many details. I did not accompany him on that trip down-river. Isn't he here now?"

Montana shook his head. "He stayed with the boat as far as Fort Benton. Said he had other business to attend to."

He had an increasingly uneasy feeling that there was more to this than misunderstanding. What Tiller-Parsons chose to do was of course his own affair, but each new report on the man was less favorable.

Rose intended to accompany them to the

ranch, but she offered no further explanation. She made no effort to take advantage of her position by remaining aloof or demanding special privileges. Instead, she helped prepare breakfast, then rode on one of the wagons. By daylight, she was even prettier than in the fire-lit dusk, and Tim O'Donnell fetched a long sigh as he and Abbott rode out ahead.

"That sun beatin' down feels just as hot as it did yesterday, so the chances are that it's just as bright," he observed. "Only somehow I don't appreciate it quite the same." He shook his head, then squared his shoulders.

"I guess dreams—especially the pleasant sort—are generally brief and are just that—dreams. And a man can wake up when he has to go ahead with what has to be done. Still, there's times when dreamin' comes as natural as breathin'."

He was silent for a long moment before ending his thought.

"But I just about stopped doin' even that when she proclaimed herself a lawfully wedded wife."

Montana sympathized with him. He liked this big ex-sergeant, and it was clear that the sudden materialization of so much beauty had affected him. Unlike Tiller-Parsons, O'Donnell was no ladies' man. For him to look twice at the same woman would be something of a record. Abbott changed the subject.

"You noticed what that outlaw had to say last evening about the trail herd?"

O'Donnell removed his hat to scratch his head. He resettled the hat at a rakish angle, a perplexed look on his face.

"Yeah, I heard. Seemed like he felt he had to explain himself. Could be he knew something, I suppose. There was some trouble with the herd, Jones being killed and so on. But what might have happened along the trail wasn't our business at the ranch or known to us. The only thing I can say for sure about that herd is that there's three thousand head of them, and they're better than average stock."

The dying man's suggestion that the herd had been rustled rather than rounded up or purchased, taken over through a deliberate massacre so as to leave no witnesses, was serious. Such a statement, made as a dying declaration, could not lightly be disregarded. On the other hand, he had been an outlaw himself, and he might have believed a report which was more malicious than accurate.

To Montana, the double-barreled name of Tiller-Parsons sounded affected if not pretentious. He wondered if, with its suggestion of prestige and family, it might have helped influence the members of the syndicate in their choice of him as manager of their American properties. Their standards for judging would hardly match those of Tim O'Donnell.

The increasingly big question, with each fresh disclosure, was why? The chartered river boat, the big beef herd, the freight which they were transporting, all proved that the financial backing for the enterprise was ample. As manager for the syndicate, there would be no point in Tiller-Parsons resorting to dishonesty, but every reason he should not. Also, it was unlikely that men of position would place the handling of their resources in his hands without first checking carefully.

The scope of the operation had appealed to Montana, and its overseas backing had seemed to assure a solid background. In any case, he decided, having taken the job, along with an advance in pay, he would be foolish to shy at shadows. If later on he didn't like the job, he could always quit.

Rose was no chatterbox. Seated beside him that afternoon while Montana drove one of the wagons, she seemed composed, slightly pensive. But she volunteered nothing more than what had already been said, and he did not ask.

They followed a wheel trace which might soon develop into a road. Ranch headquarters came in sight on the afternoon of the third day. Montana studied the setting in surprise and approval. If Tiller-Parsons had picked the site, he had shown good taste.

A house such as might grace a country estate two thousand miles to the east was in the process of being erected, with workmen busily hammering and sawing. A big barn thrust arrogantly above lesser outbuildings. Montana noted that, quite properly, the first priority had been given to structures required for the efficient operation of the ranch.

These nestled in a little valley, fringed on two sides by massive cottonwoods which were watered by a slow-running creek. Twin corrals had been built to hold the horses, their poles making a checkerboard pattern of sun and shade.

The big house was set apart, long and wide rather than high. Peeled logs gleamed, with the imported lumber being used for roofing, floors, windows and a wide porch.

Cattle grazed in the distance, as though this had been home for more than a few uneasy days.

At their approach, a tight-jawed man left the house and advanced to meet them. O'Donnell explained:

"That's Jim Anderson, in charge of the carpenters. He's a good man—though it don't look like they've gotten much done since I left here the other day."

"You're right, Mr. O'Donnell; we've accomplished next to nothing," Anderson declared heatedly. "I'm at my wits' end, and near the end of my patience as well, with a crew made stupid by booze."

"Booze?" O'Donnell repeated. "I didn't know there was any of the stuff closer than Benton. Jim, this is Montana Abbott—the new foreman, in charge during Tiller-Parsons' absence."

Anderson surveyed Montana with sharply grudging appraisal. Clearly the name meant nothing.

"It's about time that we had somebody in charge," he growled. "My only authority is to see that the carpentry work is done right, and with no one to back me or throw the fear of the devil into some of that crew, that has been no cinch. There was no liquor, but some turned up almost as soon as you fellows were out of sight. There were jugs and bottles, filled with rotgut enough to stock a saloon. The crew found them before I did, as was no doubt intended, and by the time I realized what was going on, they were drunk. They've been guzzling the stuff ever since, paying no attention to me. And the work's at a standstill."

The former sergeant shook his head, but eyed them with an understanding gaze.

"That's not so good. But they've worked hard and well for a long stint, Jim. It's in the nature of such men to go on a spree every so often."

"Sure, but not to have the stuff dropped right in their hands by someone who wants to hinder the work," Anderson pointed out. "That whisky didn't get where they couldn't help finding it by accident."

"Well, if they've been drinking the way you say, the supply should soon be running low," O'Donnell suggested philosophically.

"That's what I've been counting on. They are next to worthless until they sober up."

He paused as someone gave a delighted, if somewhat maudlin whoop. It was echoed by the others as they turned, then crowded around him. Montana pushed forward for a look, the others at his heels.

If the original supply of liquor had been running low, now it had been almost magically replenished, or so it seemed to them. Going after a board, the man had lifted it from where it lay on the ground a little to one side. Under it was a freshly dug trench filled end to end with more jugs and bottles.

To the men, this was a gift to use and enjoy, with no questions asked. The possibility that the cache might not be intended for them was not troubling their minds. Here again was largesse, to be accepted and made the most of. Bottles were being opened and upended. Anderson's shrill wail of anger and dismay was ignored. As he persisted, one man placed a big hand on his chest and shoved. Taken off balance, Anderson went down.

"Jus' cause you don't like the stuff's no reason to spoil our fun," the other man chided. "We do like—"

The smash of a bottle, coupled with the roar of the revolver in Montana's hand, startled them to bewildered attention. The slivered flask, disintegrating as it was upended, showered half the group.

"What's going on?" the dazed carpenter protested. Then anger flared in already reddened eyes as his bemused mind grasped cause and effect. "What the devil do you think you're up to?" he demanded.

"You fellows are here to work, not to drink," Montana informed him shortly. "Smash those bottles right where they are. Every one!"

This was trouble of an unlooked-for nature. Someone clearly was out to delay the work on the house, to obstruct the operations of the syndicate. Difficulties of this sort were an old story.

The sodden workmen eyed him resentfully, but before the gun and the sharpness of his tone, they offered no further protest, as Anderson and O'Donnell caught up hammers and smashed the jugs and bottles. Their sorrowing glances confirmed their opinion that this was a waste if not a desecration, but since the liquor had been an unexpected boon in the first place, the loss was not too personal.

"Montana Abbott's foreman here, and what he say goes," O'Donnell explained. "It's a point to keep in mind."

"You men are hired to work," Montana reminded them. "You might as well knock off for the day. Get some sleep, and be ready to get at it again tomorrow. One other thing. If any more of this stuff turns up, show it to me first! I'll deal personally with any man who takes another drink until this job is finished!"

What that deal might amount to, he did not elaborate, but from the nervously respectful glances bent upon him as the men shuffled off, it was clear that he had impressed them.

V

Montana was impressed in his turn. This ranch had a great potential, and undoubtedly much of the credit belonged to Tiller-Parsons. What had been done required imagination as well as ability.

He had a look at the herd the next day, and here was more proof of selectivity. They were longhorns, almost as strange to that range as its owners would be, but there was a wide difference between cattle from so vast a state as Texas. Some had run wild for generations, reverting almost to the savage, creatures of bone and horn, lean and rangy and tough and stringy as to meat. Others had retained a natural sleekness, despite necessary fighting qualities.

These were above the average for a beef herd, about evenly divided between cows and steers, but dry cows had been selected for the long trail, without calves to tag along. In consequence, they were as sleek as the steers. Now they were putting on fat on the rich grasses which were being cured in the sun.

Intrigued, Montana had a look at the books in the office. Since these were piled on a desk, instead of under lock and key, he felt that as foreman he should be familiar with them. He found what he sought, and everything seemed to be in order. But certain details made him wonder.

It was still possible, as it had been during the war years, for a crew to go into the bush country, along some of the back-country reaches of the Lone Star State, and to round up a bunch of mavericks, establishing ownership by applying their own brand. The syndicate ranch had been more businesslike as well as selective. Papers testified that this herd had been purchased from a local owner for eighteen thousand dollars, paid in cash.

That seemed a fair price for such stock, since prices were beginning to rise as twin lines of steel opened up the heartland of America. Yet in it was a smell of extravagance. A good crew could have had such stock almost for the cost of wages.

Apparently the syndicate was owned by wealthy men, and Henry Tiller-Parsons had no hesitation when it came to spending their money.

Whatever else he might be, Tiller-Parsons was a student of character, at least reasonably familiar with the class of men who employed him. Also, it seemed a fair guess that he had added either the Tiller or the Parsons to his own name, believing that a double-barreled moniker would impress them.

Which is likely his notion of giving them value received for their money, Montana decided sardonically. He had yet to find the vitally important answer to the riddle. A man might be extravagant yet basically honest, and do an excellent job. Or this might be larceny with a high polish.

Even these papers might be faked. Though properly signed and witnessed, they had not been notarized. The average buyer or seller would accept them at face value, especially since Montana was a long way from Texas.

On the whole, it appeared that a good beginning was being made at establishing the ranch and its basic commodity of meat. Yet it was a start which, even with the best of intentions, might end in catastrophe, due to a lack of foresight and experience.

The difference lay in the difference between Texas and Montana.

In their native state, running half-wild, the cattle could not only survive against odds, but flourish. Northers did sweep portions of the country, with heavy snow and blizzard cold, but they were infrequent, and normally of brief duration. Even a heavy fall of snow would usually melt soon enough so that hungry animals could feed again.

The plains and hills of southeastern Montana were a different story. The grass was shorter, less lush, but such deficiencies were compensated for by its quality of rich nourishment. Here the heat of summer could be almost as intense, but the cold of winter was longer, more enduring. Without additional care, Texas cattle could hardly hope to survive.

That was the immediate problem. Tiller-Parsons was perhaps assuming that the cattle could look after themselves as they would in Texas. So no grass had been cut for hay, and no hay would be obtainable, at any price, unless they put it up themselves.

It was already too late to do much about that. Summer was well advanced, and the chill which betokened the approach of autumn knifed the air with each dawn. However benign the summer, winter could pounce fast and hard.

An examination of the supplies on hand was partially reassuring. Montana found two scythes, the questioning of the crew elicited the information that a couple of the men had had at least a limited experience with swinging a scythe. While not too happy at the change in occupation, they set to work as he directed, where the grass stood tall and untouched in the meadows. It was browning, sun-cured as it stood.

Two men with scythes would be able to cut enough hay to carry the horses through the winter. The irony was that horses could and would forage for themselves, where cattle would not.

The carpenters, sober now, were making use of the lumber brought in on the Star of the West. Outwardly, the ranch was a beehive of activity. Yet aside from the house, there was little productivity.

"You've sure got them working," O'Donnell observed. "Everybody busy as bees."

But there was a difference in bees, Montana reflected. Honey bees stored provisions against the coming winter. Bumblebees bumbled—and accomplished nothing.

He could not rid himself of the feeling that the pattern had been deliberately set up that way, that the Powder River Ranch, for all its outward appearance, was a place of contradictions.

"I may be borrowing trouble, imagining things," he admitted. "But if it turns out that way, I could turn out to be the man in the middle—the one that gets stepped on."

Feeling a strong aversion to such a role, he set out again to ride more widely, to take a comprehensive look and familiarize himself with the ranch and with conditions. In any case, that was a necessary part of his job.

Circling beyond the cattle, which were scattered over a wide area, he came to territory that seemed as remote and lonely as might be found anywhere. But it was there, extremely surprising in such a place, that he came upon a trail, as remarkable for its freshness as that it should be there at all.

At first glance it was seemingly only a set of wheel tracks, a wagon drawn by a team of horses. In settled country, or along a road, that would excite no suspicion. Here it seemed alien; moreover, the depth to which the wheels had sunk where the soil was light and the grass scanty suggested a rather heavy load.

Even more odd, the equipage had moved to make a V—heading toward the ranch buildings, then halting and swinging off at another angle, almost directly away from the headquarters, but not retracing its former course.

Moreover, the wagon had been there very recently, probably that same day. Montana followed.

His speed would be several times that of a plodding team dragging a laden wagon. He had ridden less than an hour when he sighted the wagon ahead, and another quarter-hour was enough to catch up.

Though it had a canvas top, weathered and stained, it was in no sense a prairie schooner or covered wagon. This was an equipage not often seen so far west of the river, a light spring wagon, pulled by a tired team of ponies, who in size and build seemed more suited to the saddle than to such a chore.

A lone man perched on the seat, eying Montana with wary suspicion as he approached. A stubble of salt and pepper whiskers splotched his face, his jaws moving mechanically above a chew of tobacco, whose juices seeped like the overflow of a creek from the edges of his mouth. A Sharp's buffalo gun was on the seat beside him.

He was clearly of two minds as to what course he should pursue, but his horses solved the matter by halting of their own accord, glad of an excuse. Pale eyes surveyed Abbott, and his nod was as jerky as the jump of a frightened rabbit.

"Howdy!"

"Howdy," Montana returned, and matched the other's stare unblinkingly.

The wagoner endured its challenge for a space of heartbeats. Then he squirmed uncomfortably, loosing a stream of tobacco juice over the right front wheel.

"You want something?"

"Kind of like to satisfy my curiosity," Montana admitted. "I'm wondering what you're doing out here and what you're hauling."

There was another speculative period, while the eyes ranged the holstered gun at Montana's side, the calmly waiting face above. The man sighed resignedly.

"I ain't got nothing to hide. Besides, it's a free country—or so I've heard."

Montana's nod was noncommittal. Riding closer, he lifted the loose rear flap of the canvas and peered into the murky interior. He was not much surprised at the array of jugs and bottles, carefully packed against the jolting of the wagon. They were similar to the cache which the delighted carpenters had discovered.

Montana allowed the flap to fall. "You changed your mind?" he suggested.

"A man's got a right to, ain't he?"

"No law against it. What I'm curious about is why you were giving away good liquor in the first place without even asking credit."

"No law against that either, is there?"

"That could depend. You wanted to get those boys drunk, and you did. Went to a lot of trouble to do it. Why?"

"I was hired to."

"Makes rather a reverse twist," Abbott conceded. "Usually whisky is a big-profit deal. Furnishing it for free don't often happen."

"I guess I might as well tell you," the other man said resignedly. "One of the fellers that was murdered down Wind River way was my pard. I couldn't fight back, not the way your crew does. But he cashed in with a wad of money in his pocket. I don't know whether he had any folks anywhere or not. He never said. Anyhow, I couldn't send it to them, but I thought of this way to use it. Maybe I'd botch things up with that house, with a bunch of drunks on the job. Sure, I guess it was a crazy notion."

"You figure the Powder River crew had a hand in what happened at Wind River?"

The mottled face darkened.

"What happened there was murder. And where does the herd end up? What the devil should a man figure?"

Reduced to so simple a philosophy, it was damaging—but there were middlemen among outlaws as among honest men. An opinion, however disturbing, was not proof.

"So you decided to heap coals of fire, eh?" The blankness in the pale eyes told him that the man did not understand. "You've enough rotgut left to go into business for yourself."

A cunning gleam replaced the blankness as the driver chirped the horses into motion.

"Yeah, that's a notion. I might just do that."

VI

The long days of summer were giving way to the shorter ones of autumn. The leaves on trees and shrubs seemed to have absorbed the color if not the warmth of the sun. Birds, having sung themselves out, swept by in increasing flocks. The moon of harvest flamed nightly against wide horizons.

Tiller-Parsons, heading ranchward across-country, traveling with a retinue of horses, vehicles and men in almost princely fashion, was elated. His plans were working out excellently, as was attested to by the fact Alicia Fredericks now journeyed with him, rather than he with her. By such phrasing, he felt, was marked the change in his life, a demarcation from a period which he would as soon forget. He had been an overseer, a hired hand. Technically it was still that way, but actually he was taking an ever firmer grip on the reins.

From Fort Benton, as the Star of the West turned back down-river, he had forwarded glowing reports to the members of the syndicate, outlining accomplishments achieved or in the process of building, achievements which should leave them well satisfied. By the following summer, should some of them take the notion to risk a sea voyage and see the ranch for themselves, fantasy might almost have become fact. By then everything would be ready for them.

The early dusk had closed down, with the sun setting in what, on another night, Alicia had described as a blaze of glory. He had agreed, reflecting with some wonder that all women seemed to have romantic notions and a disposition to indulge in flights of fancy. Certainly it was pretty enough; still, a sunset was merely a going down of the sun. It was like lumping two names together to form Tiller-Parsons, a lot of foolishness, to be indulged in only because a hyphenated name seemed to impress some people.

The sudden sunset had caught him some distance from the evening camp, strolling by himself as he awaited the call to supper. Alicia usually walked with him, but tonight she had been busy with a womanly chore, that of washing and putting up her hair.

"Since we're due to reach the ranch tomorrow, I want to look my best," she had explained, and he had agreed helplessly, refraining from remarking that none of the cowboys or other hands would know the difference in any case.

Shadowy figures were suddenly all around him, emerging from the gloom like phantoms. Two men seized his arms from either side. His sharp exclamation was cut off as a hand clapped heavily over his mouth.

Struggling, as he quickly discovered, was useless. His lively fears were only slightly eased as he realized that his captors were Indians. He had been convinced that he and his party were totally alone on the prairie, that there was no risk. Even if enemies should lurk nearby, they were a large enough group to put up a good fight.

Whatever his shortcomings, Hank Tiller had never been lacking in courage. He took a grip on himself and, allowed to speak, ventured a remonstrance which he hardly hoped would prevail.

"You fellows are making a mistake. I'm your friend—Chief Spotted Pony is my friend. I want to talk to him."

One of his captors laughed, a loose, foolish gurgle. The other nodded ponderously.

"Spotted Pony—waiting."

The quality of the laugh and speech, as well as the alcoholic breaths, staggered him. These men were drunk. Not totally so, however, since an Indian, unused to hard liquor, was apt to pass out completely when such a stage was reached. But they were drunk enough to be maudlin, a good-natured phase. The trouble was that such moods could change to ugliness in a hurry.

They did not have far to go. Firelight glowed as they reached the rim of a coulee, and from its depths several figures wavered, ghost-like. The fire was reflected from flasks scattered about.

One of the men was the chief. Recognizing him, Tiller-Parsons made up his mind. He'd take a hard line, as became his position.

That might or might not be the proper way to handle Indians. Actually, he didn't know much about them, or how one was supposed to deal with them. But he did know that Spotted Pony was a chief, though with only a handful of followers. If he recollected correctly, he was supposedly friendly to white men. They had met some months before, even indulging in a game of poker.

Poker was Tiller-Parsons' greatest delight

or affliction. Where some men would get drunk whenever the opportunity presented itself, he would play the game, for increasingly high stakes. Often he won. More frequently he lost. In fact, this potbellied savage had beaten him, to the tune of a thousand dollars.

Since Spotted Pony had attended a white man's school, some of his skill in the white man's vices was understandable.

"Hi, Spotted Pony," Tiller-Parsons greeted him. His tone sharpened. "What's the idea of treating me as though I were a prisoner?"

For a long moment the chief regarded him woodenly. It was more than the reflected light of the fire. His eyes were bloodshot; his manner, like his hair, rough. He was clearly as drunk as his followers, enough to be unpredictable or ugly. Evidently this drinking bout had been going on for days.

"You are a prisoner," Spotted Pony returned insolently, but he spoke English. When sober, he was likely to insist on Indian ways, proceeding formally through an interpreter. Now he disdained such methods.

"Why do you think I've had you brought

here?" he added. The unwashed smells of camp and tepee made a rank emanation.

Tiller-Parsons' nerves stretched like drying buckskin. This had all the elements of trouble, and he had blundered straight into it. It could mean disaster, not only for himself, but for Alicia as well. But to back down would only make matters worse.

"I suppose you want another poker game," he suggested, and shrugged. "What's got into you, Chief? You're drunk."

Spotted Pony regarded him owlishly. But it was the right approach. An Indian respected courage.

"Sure I'm drunk," he acknowledged, attempting to speak carefully, though the words were slurred. Remote contempt veiled his eyes. "Why not, when white men are such fools?"

Tiller-Parsons sensed that more was back of this than he had suspected. He took a familiar tone.

"Are they? Some whites are, and so are some red men. Not you or I, though. Tell me about it. Let's sit down and get this straightened out. You know that I'm your friend, Spotted Pony."

The chief hesitated, his mood was wavering as a feather in the wind. Then he grunted and sat down, cross-legged. Relieved, Tiller-Parsons did the same.

"I've been away," he confided. "A long journey, far down the rivers. I'm just getting back. But what's this about whisky?"

The recollection had amused the chief. He was enjoying not only the fruits of his recent action but also the triumph, in retrospect.

"White men are fools," he repeated. "Did you not send this one to trade with us, to get us drunk so that we could be played with as a child plays with a toy bow? He had a wagon loaded with whisky. But instead of paying a big price for only a few drinks of it, we had it all, and at no cost. Now one of my braves has a new trophy in his scalp-lock."

That final reference was as mocking as it was challenging, but Tiller-Parsons disregarded it. Someone had gotten the notion of trading liquor to the Indians, and for his pains he had been killed and robbed. Dead, he was past helping, nor could he offer any contradiction to whatever story they chose to tell. Here again the mood of the chief was lightly balanced, ready to veer either way.

A poker player by instinct as well as liking, Tiller-Parsons knew when to gamble.

"You guessed right, Chief." He shrugged. "He was my man. Only you made a mistake. I was sending him to you with many bottles, as a gift, a token of friendship and respect. Not to trade, but to show my regard.

"You and I met a long way from here, and we had a friendly game of poker. Now, I run a ranch in this country for men who live far across the big water. So when I was told that you were now in my part of the country, I remembered how pleasant is a meeting between friends and sent him. A mistake was made, but it was not mine. Still, what is done is done. At least you received the gift."

To excuse an error which had caused a man to die sounded magnanimous. Sober, Spotted Pony would be too shrewd for such sophistry, but drunk as he was, it might work. Tiller-Parsons held his breath.

The chief pondered owlishly. Then he nodded. The mistake, being past and beyond changing, was of no consequence. But the story had a reasonable quality; it was logical to send a gift to assure his friendship. Moreover, it had an imaginative quality, such as few white men would dare. Whites usually used whisky only for trading, for cheating and debauchery.

He flung an arm across his companion's shoulders. Tiller-Parsons managed not to flinch.

"I am sorry for the mistake," Spotted Pony proclaimed. "It was a fine gift. We have enjoyed it."

Whether or not the last of the liquor had been imbibed, Tiller-Parsons noted that the Indian did not invite him to have a drink to seal the pact. Considering the circumstances, he was as well pleased. A clear mind was vital.

"What is past is past," he repeated. "Since you received and enjoyed the gift, that is all that matters. There will be other tokens of my friendship in days to come; days which may prove profitable for both of us, my friend."

VII

Work on the big house was coming along nicely. Sober again, and somewhat ashamed of their prolonged drunk, the carpenters exerted themselves to make up for the lapse. Under the supervision of Jim Anderson, they did in excellent job. Montana was more than a little amazed at the structure taking shape so far from any town, in the heart of a wilderness. Henry Tiller-Parsons might be lavish in the spending of his employers' money, but at least he would have something to show for the expenditures.

The harvesting was also doing as well as he had hoped. Several small stacks of hay had been put up, carefully fenced against forays by the herd or from deer or elk. It would not be enough to tide such a bunch of cattle over the winter, but it would be an excellent hedge against the cold for the horses.

On the whole, Montana was finding the job to his liking. Big already, there was the promise of steady enlargement. Ranching on the scale of the syndicate could be fun. With proper management and a bit of luck, it might even prove profitable for the stockholders.

Some disquieting doubts had been raised, but there might be good answers to them. Until those were provided, he could hardly do less than give his employers the benefit of the doubt.

There had been no further word from Tiller-Parsons, no contacts with the outside world. Montana had an idea that the manager would probably be turning up one of these days. When he arrived, he should be pleased with what had been accomplished.

The nearest thing to a reminder of the outside world had been a few distant smudges of smoke glimpsed on the far horizon. In reality they were not much more than wisps, not signals, but suggesting a possible Indian encampment. That was both reasonable and likely, and as long as there was no hostility from whatever wandering band might be off there, there was no cause for worry.

Tim O'Donnell concurred with his opinion.

"Indians, more than likely. There are other outfits of white men no more'n a day's ride from here, and that could be from some of them, but more likely it'd be Spotted Pony's band. He's a Piegan, kind of a lone wolf. Not exactly a trouble-maker, maybe—but he'll bear watching."

The extent of the supplies which had been planned, purchased, then transported some two thousand miles and were now going into the house was astonishing. Not only were there several glass windows, but some of the glass was colored. Other touches, such as square white pillars for the porch, were equally luxurious. Powder River Ranch was intended to vie with English estates. Tiller-Parsons intended not only to impress his employers when they should eventually pay a visit to their holdings, but to make them feel at home.

There was much which was right here, and only one thing which seriously troubled him. That was Rose Tiller-Parsons, as she had proclaimed herself to be, and how Tiller-Parsons might feel about her presence when he arrived. During the interim, there had been no real problem. Mrs. Sally Miller was the housekeeper, a competent, bustling lady, settled in a small adjoining house prior to Montana's arrival. Such a place as was being built would require the service of someone like her, and Tiller-Parsons had not overlooked that angle.

Upon Mrs. Miller's invitation, Rose had moved in with her, pending the completion of the big house and the arrival of Tiller-Parsons. The two women had become fast friends.

If Montana was apprehensive on general principles, Tim O'Donnell was even more troubled, and more personally. He expressed his feelings with some heat.

"'The little lady's an angel, Montana—as fine as they come, and on that I'll stake a stack of blues! She's as quiet and tidy as a brown grouse, but what she is just sort of shines! Which leaves us up against the rest of it—and that beats me; I just can't figure matters."

Montana elevated a quizzical eyebrow.

"You're suggesting that Tiller-Parsons may not be equally angelic?"

The reply was explosive.

"Him! All I know for sure—beyond my remarks concernin' her—is that I'm a fool. Was I any less a one, I'd be pullin' stakes and betakin' myself to a far country, beyond the bewitchin' glance of such a pair of eyes! But I'm intrigued to discover certain answers which'll sooner or later be forthcomin'. And who knows? When that time comes, she might even need a friend."

"In which case you'll be around."

"In which case I'll sure enough be around," O'Donnell agreed emphatically.

They were riding together, somewhat farther afield than usual. Lacking a survey, which would probably be far in the future, no one, Montana included, had any firm idea regarding the boundaries of Powder River Ranch. Such descriptions as he had found among the papers were grandiose but vague. And the lines did not matter too much, as long as the country remained uncrowded.

But sooner or later others would come, and when that day arrived, familiarity with the range would be vital. Whether or not he would be there then Montana had no way of knowing, but as long as he was foreman, he wanted a working knowledge of the territory.

It was off in this section that he had encountered the man with his wagon and stock of liquor some time before. Whether or not he'd realized it, whisky could be a dangerous cargo.

O'Donnell was staring into the distance, shading his eyes with a hand against the sun.

"Something sort of odd off there," he suggested. "Something that don't quite fit."

Montana had noticed it also. As they drew nearer, the strangeness became understandable. The thing had once been a wagon, the light spring type, next to a saddle pony the fastest means of transportation available. Now there remained only a charred and twisted wreckage, a lonely hulk which seemed to crouch close to the ground as though to hide its shame, perhaps cowering in terror.

The wooden parts, including the box and running gear, along with the spokes of the wheels, had been pretty well consumed. Tire irons and metal parts remained. The grass had been consumed close to and around the wagon, but in still green grass the fire had not edged far beyond. Since the fire, rain had caused a thin new growth to tint the blackened area with its freshness.

Still, this fire and destruction were of recent origin. Montana was not positive, but he felt reasonably certain that this was the wagon he had seen before.

One broken bottle lay among the ashes. There was no sign of the team or the driver.

"Everything looks mighty peaceful as of now," O'Donnell observed, his gaze ranging the horizon. "But appearances can be as deceivin' as judgin' from a frog's looks which way he'll jump.'

Abbott explained his encounter, the reason for the load of liquor and the new purpose for which it had been intended. He drew no conclusions, but with the ex-sergeant a blueprint was unnecessary.

"One time in a book, I got to readin' about termites," O'Donnell murmured.

"Seems they're sort of a little bug that likes to eat wood. An old house can be full of such critters without nobody even suspectin' it, till one day the place comes clatterin' down about your ears; what you'd call a case of being et out of house and home. Ain't a thing to see here, neither—but such varmints as you don't see can be as obnoxious as the kind that barge in and outstay their welcome."

"What do you know about these neighbors of ours?" Montana asked.

"They're part of the larger tribe of Blackfeet, a sort of independent bunch under Spotted Pony. I gather that he carries a grudge against just about everybody, whites in particular. Somebody got hold of him as a boy and sent him off to a mission school. Trained him like a white man—only it didn't take. Or maybe it did. Learned all our bad tricks on top of his own. This could be his work."

The Blackfeet had always been independent, generally distrustful of the white man. That they had been given reason enough for such an attitude over the years, Montana was not inclined to dispute. Probably Spotted Pony was no worse a neighbor than most, but the wreckage of the wagon was a warning to keep in mind.

"Makes me shiver," O'Donnell observed, breaking a long silence. They were halfway back to the ranch buildings. "I cain't get out of my mind about Rose—Mis' Tiller-Parsons—turnin' up all by herself, out of nowhere, like she did. I reckon where she came from and what she does is *her* business—it sure ain't mine. But sashayin' around alone in such country ain't what I'd recommend as healthy. A wife ought to be with her husband," he concluded violently, "special if she's going to travel in country such as this! What's a man thinkin' of to let her go without him?"

As they topped a slope, the headquarters came into sight. The house was taking on an air of livability. Inside and out, finishing touches were being applied, and the over-all effect was impressive. The owners would be hard to please if they did not approve, while as for a woman—

For the twentieth time, Montana found himself wondering what Alicia Fredericks would think, since her position in Eastern society had obviously entitled her to move in exalted circles. And as for Rose—

Montana had asked no questions, nor had

she volunteered any additional information concerning herself or her claim. Living with the housekeeper, she had quietly assumed the place of mistress, as wife of the ranch manager. But she made no demands, advanced no claims. Yet answers would have to be forthcoming presently.

Anderson reported the job finished. Together they inspected the work of a spring, summer and early fall. The carpenters' foreman was justifiably proud.

"It's the biggest job I've ever worked on," he admitted, "and one of the fanciest. This house is the sort that you'd expect to find in upstate New York or New England, or down South before the war. Out here—well, I'll confess that it is beyond my understanding, but that's not my affair. I hope somebody gets some good out of it."

Like his crew, he was anxious to get away, to make the trek back to civilization before the coming of winter. Montana paid them off, as Tiller-Parsons had arranged if they left before his return. In addition to the barn, bunkhouse and cook house, three small guest houses had been erected. Without the clatter of hammers and saws, the cluster of buildings seemed suddenly silent, a lonely oasis in the wilderness.

The term was hardly an exaggeration. The gold camps of Helena, Diamond City, Virginia City or Bannack were flourishing centers, and a few other settlements, including Fort Benton, had their reasons for being. Also, some ranches were being established. But for the most part Montana remained a wide and lonely territory, no section more so than this one along the Powder River.

With a comfortably substantial headquarters established, the English syndicate was, at least theoretically, in a position to exploit the situation, to build big. And if this house was a fair indication of what Tiller-Parsons could do, it might come to pass.

Montana felt a loyalty to the outfit, to his absent employers. He wanted to see the venture succeed. But the future of the ranch was in the hands of the manager and, to say the least, Tiller-Parsons seemed to be taking his responsibilities lightly.

One of the cowboys rode in to report he had sighted a small caravan of horses and wagons trekking steadily toward the headquarters; also a single-seated, high-topped buggy, drawn by a team of matched ponies.

"Reckon you'll want to sort of have a welcomin' committee," he added, grinning broadly. "I hustled to let you know."

Rose appeared at the corner of the house, listening. As usual, she was neat, as unobtrusive as a beautiful woman could hope to be, asking no questions, volunteering nothing. But the usual color had fled her cheeks, leaving them as stark as frost at dawn.

She don't know what to expect, Montana thought, considering that buggy with its fancy team. And neither do I.

They would not be long now in finding out. The wagons were in sight, a considerable amount of freight and supplies, obviously being brought against the needs of the coming winter. Tiller-Parsons had not overlooked the welfare of the ranch.

The buggy was in the lead, the team coming on at a swinging trot. Red wheels flashed in the sun. Then the horses were pulled up with a flourish along the curving driveway, the wheels cramped open with easy skill. Wrapping the reins about the whipstock, Tiller-Parsons jumped down and hurried around to assist his companion, extending both arms. Montana and O'Donnell recognized her without surprise. Eyes sparkling, with vivid color whipped into her cheeks, Alicia Fredericks was gazing about eagerly.

Tiller-Parsons held her a moment longer than was necessary, then set her on her feet, turning with a broad smile.

"Welcome home, my dear," he said. "Folks, allow me to introduce my wife, Mrs. Tiller-Parsons!"

VIII

The words fell like a cold breeze, though Montana was hardly surprised. Tiller-Parsons' conduct was like a well-woven piece of tapestry. But again and again the precise pattern was disturbed by irregularities.

Nearly all of the ranch hands had gathered, eager to welcome their boss, as much because of the break which his arrival afforded in the monotony as anything else. Most of them enjoyed working for the syndicate. Powder River Ranch was remote, but the accommodations were comfortable and the food better than average. For so big a crew, the work was light, with few of the usual chores to be found on a big spread. There had been no fall roundup, no branding. Such work as was necessary could be done by a third as many men. Montana suspected that the extra hands were for protection against possible Indian attacks.

At Tiller-Parsons' announcement, they stared, slack-jawed, wondering if they had heard aright. The radiant look on the face of Alicia convinced them.

Rose was standing frozen, her face drained of color.

The booming welcome which the crew had intended to provide failed to erupt. It was Timothy O'Donnell, a hard undercurrent of anger in his voice, who broke the silence.

"Mrs. Tiller-Parsons, you say? Now how in the devil can that be, with Mrs. Tiller-Parsons aleady here?"

The chopping gesture of one big hand took in Rose, leaving no doubt as to his meaning.

The rich autumnal color faded from Alicia's cheeks, as color faded from a flower at the touch of frost. She gazed around, hurt and bewildered, then looked at Tiller-Parsons for an explanation and reassurance. Neither was in his face. Surprise, consternation, disbelief and horror made a mixture which left him temporarily wordless. He had been taken completely off guard.

He stared at Rose, at least as surprised as

Montana had been when she had first appeared. Anger and contempt blazed in her eyes, but she did not seem to share the universal surprise.

Tiller-Parsons swallowed, but Montana gave him credit for courage. Faced with a crisis which not only spoiled his triumphant homecoming but threatened his career, his recovery was swift.

"Mrs. Tiller-Parsons?" he repeated, and the blankness on his face was gradually replaced by an excellent approximation of amazement. "I'm afraid I don't understand. There's some mistake here—there has to be." He bowed to Rose with stiff formality. "I have never seen this lady before."

Alicia had been about to question him, but she stood silent, still holding onto his arm, looking from one to another, as much doubt as bewilderment in her eyes. A touch of color returned to Rose's cheeks, and she took a step toward them.

"So you disown me now—after robbing, then deserting me? After that, I'm not too surprised. But I am no less your wife."

A pained look pinched the brow over the pale eyes of Tiller-Parsons.

"I'm sorry," he said, and spread both hands in a wide, disarming gesture. "Obviously there is some mistake, some misunderstanding." Then his face darkened at the gaping interest of the crew.

"Whatever it is, let us discuss it in private and reasonably," he added. "I'm happy to be back—or at least I was. But I'm sure you men have work to do. These supplies need to be unloaded."

He looked at Alicia with mingled anger and contriteness.

"I'm more distressed than I can say, my dear. But this is clearly a misunderstanding, or perhaps a case of mistaken identity. Yes, that must be it—it has to be," he went on confidently. "So let us go inside and try to straighten it out. You, of course." Again he bowed to Rose. "And you, Mr. Abbott, if you will be so good."

"I'm coming, too," Tim O'Donnell growled, and placed a big hand under Rose's elbow. But she required no assistance, walking proud and straight. Tiller-Parsons favored the ex-sergeant with a sharp glance, but shrugged.

The big house was obviously ready for his arrival. The front door stood open, the housekeeper beside it. Though she had waited welcomingly, she now remained discreetly in the background. Tiller-Parsons cast a swiftly appraising glance about, but whether he was pleased or otherwise, it did not show in his face or voice. Not until all except O'Donnell were seated did he speak. O'Donnell remained grimly standing.

"You, madam—" Tiller-Parsons bowed a third time to Rose—"claim to be my wife, which is a manifest impossibility. But I'm certain that this is a case of misunderstanding or mistaken identity. If you will be so good as to give us your story—"

Rose's eyes were hot with anger, her voice brittle with scorn. Hers was the terrible quality of the aroused meek.

"There's no mistake, Henry Tiller," she said. "You married me a year and a half ago, back East, professing to love me. Fool that I was, I believed you and allowed you to get your hands on my money. As soon as you had that you walked out on me."

"Aha, money," O'Donnell cut in. "Was it a great deal now, Rose ma'am?"

"A great deal to me," Rose admitted. "Twenty thousand dollars."

"And you robbed, then deserted her—"

Tiller-Parsons' hand raised imperatively.

"I can understand your feelings," he said. "In fact, I share them. But I believe I have the explanation. Though I'm certainly not proud of it, nor have I been inclined to mention it to anyone, I have a twin brother. For most of his years he has been a ne'er-do-well type, but in appearance he is astonishingly like myself. Apparently he is not above playing so despicable a trick, even upon a woman. The only additional explanation that I can see is that he took advantage of you, madam, also of me, using my name and reputation, deceiving you, then deserting you. Certainly I do not doubt your veracity. The whole affair is extremely unfortunate."

The English had a habit of understatement, and in this he aped them. It seemed to Montana the understatement of the year.

Rose eyed Tiller-Parsons sharply, but he had implanted at least a shade of doubt.

"That's too incredible to be true," she protested.

Tiller-Parsons fetched a convincing sigh. He had found himself in tight fixes on a number of occasions, most recently when Spotted Pony had been of two minds as to whether to treat him as a friend and ally, or instead rob the supply train, acquiring a collection of hair trophies as a bonus. But with each crisis he acquired increasing adroitness.

"It does seem so," he acknowledged. "But it appears that both of us have been victimized by my scapegrace brother. Unfortunately, he is not at hand to be compelled to face up to his responsibilities. Under the circumstances, dear lady, I can only sympathize with your perfectly natural mistake. Beyond that, it seems that I have gained a sister-in-law. That being so, Alicia and I extend you our sympathy and affection, and of course our hospitality. I shall certainly attempt to locate my graceless brother and see to it that he makes restitution."

Once again, his luck had held. If the others did not entirely believe him, at least they could not disprove his version. Tiller-Parsons was sweating, but breathing more easily.

It might become necessary to change some of his long-range plans, since he must be prepared for any possible eventualities. Whatever happened, he had to keep control of the situation. His eyes seemed to grow more colorless and remote, staring speculatively into the future.

There were possibilities, means to an end, which might be used, should it be necessary; methods which would insure a permanent solution. But for the present he preferred not to think about such things.

With an abrupt change of manner, he turned to some immediate tasks. An inspection of the house brought his enthusiastic approval. Alicia, sobered by what happened, managed only a tremulous smile when he reminded her that she was now its mistress, but he knew that she was reassured as well as pleased.

"I never dreamed to find such a place, way off here," she admitted. "It's almost like a transplanted fairyland."

"I was hoping that you would like it." He smiled. "Again, I'm sorry about this other matter—sorry for everyone, for you that you had to be involved, and especially for her. The thing is monstrous."

"What I can't understand is why your brother would use your name or want to involve you," Alicia protested.

"I can understand that part only too well." Tiller-Parsons shrugged. "As I told you, he's a graceless scamp. Clearly, he married Rose only to get his hands on her money, intending to desert her once that was accomplished. By using my name and reputation, it was easier for him to manage. And once he walked away, he was in the clear."

Which, he reflected, was almost the truth. It had worked out that way, except for Rose turning up again, thousands of miles away. That was the last possibility he had ever dreamed of.

Rose was at least silenced, and he felt that he had removed Alicia's doubts. As for what the ranch crew might think, he simply did not care. In any case, it was none of their business.

Tim O'Donnell thought otherwise. He was explosively frank with Montana.

"The man's a liar and a scoundrel," he declared, "takin' advantage of trustin' women in such fashion! He's the same as saying that Rose is a liar, and that she would not do. She's not that kind of a woman."

"It's not quite that way," Montana pointed out. "If he should have a twin brother—"

"There never was a brother, and you don't believe that wild story any more than I do!"

"For the present, I'll give him the benefit of the doubt," Montana decided, "though there's a heap of doubt involved."

He rode with Tiller-Parsons the next day to look over the cattle, along with improvements of the past several weeks. He noted his quick interest in the stacks of hay, his approval of what had been done. One fact was apparent. Tiller-Parsons was well fitted for the position he held. He had ability. To what uses he turned such talent was the question that loomed increasingly large.

The haystacks served as a starting point for the problem which worried Montana most.

"Winter up here's not at all the same as down Texas way. The herd is in fine shape now—but I'm worried as to whether they can survive a Montana winter."

"You're right, of course, and I've had that on my mind. Almost as soon as I had made arrangements for the herd, I saw that it was a mistake, that we couldn't be ready to care for them properly." A sly smile lightened his face. "So I made other arrangements. There are the gold camps—where meat will be in short supply."

What he was suggesting was at least feasible. "You intend to sell them to the camps?"

"That's the general idea; only we will drive them part way to market, then turn them over to a buyer and his crew. He has agreed to pay cash for the herd, and that way, it will be his responsibility to get the cattle the rest of the way, then to turn them into beefsteaks. I always prefer to do such jobs with a minimum of risk and a maximum of profit."

It appeared that all the arrangements had been concluded. Montana would set out, with six men, to move the herd about a hundred miles, to the vicinity of Pomp's Pillar, up the valley of the Yellowstone. There, the buyer would take over.

"He will pay you cash," Tiller-Parsons emphasized. "Thirty thousand dollars. That amount will give us a substantial profit on the deal and make a nice report for the owners, eh?"

"They should be pleased," Montana ageed. It was almost too neat, with the risks of winter swept aside, and a handsome profit insured. Certainly it was bold and imaginative.

A rider had come in while they were making the inspection, bringing mail from the latest up-river boat. There were three letters from England, and these carried news which the manager found startling but not particularly unsettling. He relayed it to Montana.

"I've been meaning to tell you, Montana, how well pleased I am with what you've accomplished since taking over as foreman. With the buildings done and everything in order, we're in shape to entertain company—and that is most fortunate.

"I had been counting on some of our stockholders paying us a visit by next summer, but my reports must have been more optimistic than I intended. Or perhaps they have a feeling for adventure, and think that they'd enjoy a bit of roughing it. At any event, several of them are already on the way, to enjoy a vacation, look over their property and, as they put it, to enjoy some good hunting.

"Sir John Crispin, Mr. and Mrs. Silvanius Drew, also the Right Honorable Thomas Noonan and his lady, along with Mr. Byron Fancher, who is the London manager of the syndicate, will be here by the first possible boat up the river, which may of course well be the last of the season. We'll have to try and show them a good time."

IX

"Somehow, sir, this is all too pat—too blasted handy, the way things work out." Tim O'Donnell spoke with a restrained formality, sure proof that he was deeply troubled. A deepening friendship had developed between the two former soldiers, and the ex-sergeant was far more frank than he would ever have dreamed of being with his captain. The news concerning the herd, the buyer who would be waiting along the Yellowstone, and the coming of the owners from England served to perplex rather than reassure him.

"Tiller-Parsons prides himself on careful planning and foresight," Montana returned mildly. "And he seems to get results."

"Yeah, he does so," O'Donnell agreed gloomily. "Such planning is almost too good. I don't like the man or trust him. I'd feel better if I was going along with you to deliver that herd. I hope you'll watch your step."

Montana was genuinely amused.

"If you weren't the man you are, Tim, I'd have to accuse you of being an old maid, of seeing a ha'nt behind every bush. Seven of us are enough to move the herd for a few days, after which we'll be coming back. There's little enough risk. Besides, you and I will both feel easier in our minds, having you here to keep an eye on things."

"Well, there's that," Tim conceded. "Him treating Rose so fine, like a sister-in-law—which ain't fine at all, when the man's a bigamist, and what more there's no telling. There's just one thing I'm sure of. He's no ordinary villain."

Montana was inclined to agree. He liked the ranch and the job, but he was increasingly distrustful of the manager. Once the cattle were delivered, he would give serious consideration to moving on.

A day was spent gathering the herd. Then they set out, and the animals looked fat and sleek. No longer rangy, they plodded sedately, giving no trouble. That seemed to confirm Tiller-Parsons' judgment that seven men were a big enough crew to handle them. On the other hand, an attack such as had been made upon this herd once before could succeed more readily under such circumstances. And the bulk of the crew had been left to loiter idly at the ranch.

But nothing untoward occurred. A week brought them to the vicinity of Pomp's Pillar, that upthrust of stone which had so impressed the captains Clark and Lewis as they worked their way up the broad valley of the Yellowstone.

Horatio Gates arrived, also on schedule, with a crew of ten to take over the herd. Everything was as Tiller-Parsons had outlined, including the money. Having tallied the stock and verified the papers, Gates handed over the cash.

"Well I guess that takes care of the legal end," he observed. "We'll go on with them in the morning. Hope you have a good trip back, Abbott. May be kind of a lonely journey, all by yourself."

Here, like the far-off moan of a blizzard, was the first suggestion of trouble. Montana eyed him sharply.

"By myself? There are seven of us."

"Seven of you this far," Gates agreed blandly. "But I'm hiring your men to go on with me and help with the herd. Tiller-Parsons arranged the deal. Didn't he tell you?"

"This is the first I'd heard of it."

"That's funny. He told me it'd be a favor to him if I could give them a job. With the herd gone, he'll only need a few men on the ranch, and he wants to hold costs down, to show a profit."

On the surface, that sounded reasonable as well as logical. But why had everyone so carefully refrained from any mention of such a plan in his presence? The crew members might have supposed that he knew, but Tiller-Parsons should have explained.

It was a hundred miles back to the ranch,

and that could prove to be a lonely trail, with thirty thousand dollars to deliver at its end. Having counted on the six as a bodyguard, Montana had not been worried. But this was a horse of a different and very dark color.

The sale and delivery of the cattle had been planned well in advance, ostensibly with an eye to the oncoming winter. With every detail worked out, the heretofore casual aspects were suddenly glaringly weak. Thirty thousand was a huge sum of money to entrust to a single man across five score miles of country.

Tiller-Parsons had married Rose, gotten hold of her money, then had walked out on her. Never suspecting that she could turn up at the remote ranch, he had risked another marriage to Alicia Fredericks. And she too, it seemed, was a wealthy woman.

There was the herd, and the testimony which had been given was well above the rumor stage: that it had been obtained not by purchase, but by treachery and murder.

Now there was thirty thousand dollars in cash—which he alone was to be responsible for.

Montana had experienced too many shadows to start at one more, but the chilling part was that everything was in order, according to careful planning. If something happened, and the money was lost—

Dead, he could hardly be held responsible—but there was scant comfort in that reflection. His reputation, along with the fact he had been killed, would demonstrate that it had been a bona-fide robbery. No real blame could attach to Tiller-Parsons.

The important difference would be that the dividend would not be paid to the ranch and its owners. Instead, most of that thirty thousand would probably find its way into the private pocket of Henry Tiller-Parsons.

Montana's face betrayed none of his suspicions. But he was thinking back to the route just traversed, reviewing the miles which would lie ahead, regardless of which direction he might choose to ride. In every direction the country stretched wide and lonely. There would be plenty of time and chance for bushwhacking.

They would of course credit him with seeing the trap and trying to avoid it. So they would have planned accordingly.

It struck him that the combined crew were more than usually jovial as they ate supper and cracked jokes. He joined with the rest, betraying no outward concern, then rolled in his blankets near the remnants of the cook fire. He slept, but presently came awake as he had intended. A faint high wind rustled the leafless branches of the cottonwoods, and not far to the side the river murmured.

Snores and heavy breathing were all about him. Moving carefully, he slipped away for a hundred feet before pausing to tug on his boots. As he came erect, a prowling coyote was briefly outlined against the sheen of the river.

The herd was bedded down a mile away, one man riding night watch. Should he think, when the watch was changed, to inspect Montana's blankets, he would find them empty. But that was a small and unlikely risk which had to be taken.

The buyers had brought along a big horse remuda. Those animals, along with the mounts belonging to his own former crew, were also bedded down for the night according to individual preferences. Some stood heads down; others sprawled on the ground. As he neared them, he saw that two were awake, having grazed to the edge of the bunch. All of the animals were hobbled.

Montana chose the pair, removing their hobbles. Knowing him, they did not shy.

Riding one and driving the other, he swung away, causing no disturbance.

Circling on the back trail, he was tempted to alter course and keep going. With a change of mounts and a few hours' start, he'd stand a fifty-fifty chance over the long haul. But the certainty of pursuit, of murder once they came within rifle range, held no appeal. He was playing for better odds.

A few miles out from the camp, he hid the extra horse, picketing it among a clump of cottonwoods. Then he returned.

More than half of the night had been used up, but the men still slept, though most of the horse herd were awake and grazing. Leaving the horse he had ridden, Montana crawled into his blanket. This second nap was as brief as the first, before the stirring of others around him brought him yawningly awake.

Breakfast, like supper, was a friendly meal, the cordiality of his fellows a shade too warm, their casualness somewhat overdone. He doubted that all of them would be in on the planned operation of which he was the center, so for their benefit, things must be made to look right.

The cook smothered the remnants of his fire as packs were rolled and tied, the horses brought in and saddled. They saluted one another gravely; then the herd got under way, while he jogged in the opposite direction.

The fact that he had taken no alarm, making no effort to slip away, had made them overconfident. Apparently no one had bothered to count the remuda, to discover that one horse was missing.

Nothing was likely to happen for a while, in the full light of day, with a long trail stretched ahead. Montana took his time, the probable sequence of events reasonably certain in his mind. The terrain had pretty well fashioned that in advance, and he had a hunch that this had been taken into account when the Pillar had been chosen as the meeting place for the two crews.

At what would be a convenient distance, there was only a single good route through and among rocky, broken country; this ran for half a dozen miles. They had brought the herd along that trail, and he must use it as he returned, or swing miles out of his way, to struggle over a course at least as difficult and inhospitable.

Either way, they could follow his sign, in a perfect country for an ambush.

The likely places for a bushwhack were

about the right distance from last night's camp, so that he would pass amid the lengthening shadows of late afternoon. In this again was grim evidence of careful planning.

An occasional look behind disclosed no evidence of pursuit, nothing to excite suspicion, but he expected none. In so well-conceived a scheme for such high stakes, the bushwhackers would be a separate group, posted in advance to await his coming. That way, they could watch his movements and pick their time.

His nerves were like drying rawhide as the afternoon waned and the rough country lay ahead. He had a pretty good notion about where they might post themselves; there were two or three excellent spots. The real risk was that, weary of waiting, they might become impatient and advance the schedule.

Against that possibility he could pit only his skill and the instinct of the hunted. Fall lay across the land. Tree leaves were brown or stained to sharper tints by the frost, but were only partially swept from limbs and brush by the hungry snooping of the wind. The sun slanted with a deceptive warmth, as though denying that snow might replace it in a night. A faint haze hung in the air, lending a luminous quality.

Nothing suggested trouble as he rode. Birds and small rodents, making the most of this remnant of summer, sailed or scurried, intent upon their own affairs. A stream widened into a long marshy pond. A muskrat was busy among the reeds.

A long meadow stretched ahead, the last real open space before the rough country. A scrub of evergreens made a sharp demarcation with the cottonwoods which had claimed the wider valley. At the far side of the meadow, birds took uneasy flight—magpies, apparently disturbed by something or someone sheltered among the trees.

That was what he had been looking for. A man might yawn and stretch, but such movement would call him to the attention of the birds. His hunch seemed confirmed.

He swung aside, finding the other horse where he had left it during the night. It had grazed all available grass within the reach of the rope, and now stood with weary patience, its tail switching at flies. It welcomed him with a whicker of relief.

Having made his own plan to counter the other, Montana worked swiftly. He had already cut a convenient sapling. Now he bent it double, tying the ends to the stirrup skirts on either side of the saddle. Braced at each end from the saddle, it stuck up to the height of a seated man, and across this frame he affixed his hat and coat. At a distance it would look real enough.

The part he disliked was sending his own horse ahead along the trail. With bridle reins tied to the saddle-horn, he put it to a brisk run with a whiplash across its withers. But there was no help for this. The bushwhackers would recognize the pony and be looking for it, be posted above the trail as it came.

It might have been the dress rehearsal for a play, farce or comedy rather than tragedy, except that as the first shots rang out and the frightened pony failed to stop, the next bullets were closer, with grimmer intent. The cayuse faltered, made a wild effort, then spilled down a short, steep incline and lay still, even as the echoes of the long guns whispered to silence.

X

Such a methodical working out of the ambush was chilling, confirming as it did

Montana's own deductions and suspicions. In such a deal, no leeway was allowed for human or animal life or the quality of mercy. As far as they could plan, the bushwhackers were taking no chances.

He reflected on this almost with a sense of regret. Such ability might carry a man a long way, to great attainments. It seemed a pity that such talents were not being turned to better purpose; if not for the man himself, at least for the sake of the women who loved and trusted him.

Even the incomplete record was impressive. Hank Tiller, whose name as well as his present efforts suggested a dubious youth, had planned to better himself, socially and financially. Hank Tiller had become Henry Tiller-Parsons. He had married Rose, gotten hold of her money, then deserted her, since she had nothing more to give to further his career.

Apparently he had taken ship for England, and with ample money to bolster his new role along with an exercise of charm, he had gained his next objective. Accepted in the proper circles, he had been hired to manage the ranch for the syndicate.

With such backing, and given the spending of large sums of money, he had done a commendable job. Most men would have been satisfied to build solidly from that point, but he was not. At each turn, someone had to pay his personal account. And those payments were exacted in treachery and murder.

It was only too clear now, and loyalty to the man who had hired him was no longer involved; Tiller-Parsons had forfeited any claim to that. But loyalty to the ranch was a different matter.

One question had been puzzling: why Tiller-Parsons, playing for high stakes, should have hired him. Now he understood. Confident that his deserted wife would never find him, Tiller-Parsons had decided to risk another marriage if he could win the lady, again with the same purpose in mind—to get his hands on her money.

In order to have time for his courtship, to remain with the river boat, he had needed a replacement for the slain ranch foreman, and Montana had turned up most conveniently. He was more than handy, in that he had a reputation for honesty.

That aspect was vital to Tiller-Parsons in this particular deal, which he had already arranged. Let the cattle be sold, the cash be paid over to a man of unquestioned integrity. Whatever happened then, no lack of good intentions could very well be laid to Tiller-Parsons.

Circling, Montana came upon the bushwhackers as they were making the unpleasant discovery that the figure planted beneath the dead horse was not himself, but only his coat and hat. There were three of them, and they had ridden up, soberly enough at first, not liking their job. Picking a target at long range was more or less impersonal; they would have preferred to keep it that way, but the money had to be recovered.

One man was getting down from the saddle, moving like an old man. A second remained seated, his eyes fixed between his horse's ears. The third, untroubled by compunctions, walked across to stare down, jibing roughly at his more squeamish companions.

"What's wrong with you two? Ain't you never seen blood before? A hunk of meat's a hunk—"

Jaw slackening, he gaped as realization hit him. His companions were still uncertain as the voice of their supposed victim rapped at them from behind.

"All right, boys, hold steady! No sudden moves—that would be a mistake. After the way you've been setting an example, I might get trigger-happy!"

Carefully, on command, they lifted their guns and dropped them, then stood or sat, painfully reaching. The shock of finding their victim alive, with a full understanding of the situation, was sobering.

They were oddly assorted, but alike in one respect. Life had dealt harshly with them, as with many during the war years. The gold camps, with their remoteness from established law and the chance for easy wealth, had been a magnet for men of their type.

The camps had proved lucrative, until the Vigilantes had sent them scattering. Now they hired their guns to men who felt themselves above killing chores but did not hesitate to employ others.

Montana's anger was tempered by understanding. Such employment was akin to the hiring of mercenaries to fight a war. By whatever name, killing was a dirty business.

All three were tall. Sharp fox-eyes peered from folds of flesh in the face of the man who had been the first to dismount. A loose grin hung lopsidedly on his mouth.

"You sure enough fooled us," he observed. "But I guess it's all in the game."

"Meaning that I should shoot you and be done with it?" Montana suggested.

They blinked uncertainly. If this was a joke, they had it coming, but he might well mean it.

"Wa'n't nothin' personal in what was going on," the middle gunman protested. "We was hired to do a job. A man's got to live."

"By killing others? It's not a convincing argument, my friend, particularly with me."

One upraised hand sagged, to brush across a stubble of beard in a nervous gesture. "No, I reckon not," he conceded unhappily.

"I might be interested in who hired you," Montana offered.

The third man shrugged.

"We got some principles left," he grunted. "Get on with it."

" *'Tenshun!*" The command, barked in a drill sergeant's accents, startled two of them. The third man snapped to attention, confirming Montana's guess that he had been a soldier. He held the pose a moment, then relaxed defiantly.

"All right," Montana said sharply. "I want to know."

"Hell with you, Yank. I don't have to

answer no questions for you. I was a Reb—and proud of being one!"

"Makes two of us," Montana returned quietly. "I led a blue rescue column to save some settlers at the close of the war. It was over and lost, but they still had their lives. While the war lasted, until I was taken prisoner, I was a captain of cavalry, C. S. A."

The ex-soldier stared uncertainly, wetting his lips. "You was for the South?"

"Just as much as you." He allowed that to sink in for a moment. "We worked for the same cause then. Now we work for the same man."

"Well, maybe so, only—"

He caught himself sharply, coloring. "I ain't sayin' nothing," he ended doggedly.

Montana shrugged the disclaimer aside. The man had already said enough. There had been no doubt about them, but Montana had felt honor-bound to give Tiller-Parsons the benefit of every doubt. It was almost a new low, to hire a man so that he might be killed, branded a felon and tumbled into a dishonored grave.

Almost, but perhaps not quite. Tiller-Parsons' treatment of women was worse.

He gathered up the dropped guns, loading them into a pair of saddlebags, then mounted one of the horses.

"I'll toss out your guns after I've gone about a mile. You may need them. Sorry that you'll have to ride shanks' mares, but I need these."

The former soldier wet his lips with dawning incredulity, in slow understanding.

"You ain't aimin' to kill us?"

"That wouldn't profit anybody," Montana returned. "In any case, there's already been too much killing."

XI

To a gambler, the benefits of a poker face are many, and Tiller-Parsons not only understood but made use of them, though he thought sardonically that the debits more often than not outweighed the benefits.

There were such disadvantages as losing a fortune, virtually on the turn of a card, and betraying no emotion, not even by the quiver of an eyelash. To take such luck impassively was the mark both of an experienced card player and a sportsman. The bad part was that it had a way, when coupled with a losing tendency, to get a man in over his head, often to the point of desperation.

Since adding Parsons to his name and adopting the character which went with the new appellation, this ability had proved profitable, bringing him to his present position through contacts with men of money and prestige. That had been equally true of the ladies.

But the losses had a way of not merely offsetting, but of outrunning the gains. And in such a stratum of society, if a man was to maintain his standing, he must pay his losses, most especially those at cards.

In other words, he reflected grimly, the higher you climbed, the farther you fell. It tempted a man to go back to the more direct, simpler ways of straight banditry.

At this stage of his career he should be rich, instead of teetering constantly on the brink of disaster. Three separate times when he was threatened with ruin, women had come, however unwittingly, to his rescue. Yet even with such windfalls, and other deals such as the cut he would receive from the sale of the beef herd, he was far from being in the winner's circle.

Now he pondered, considering a few remarks that he had chanced to overhear. The chance had been brought about by carefully putting himself in a position to eavesdrop, which occasioned him embarrassment only in what it disclosed. Timothy O'Donnell had been speaking to Rose, his voice restrained but insistent.

"The Indians call this the harvest moon, and it used to be my favorite time of the year," he observed. "But these mornings, there's a smell in the air. The stench of polecat comes and goes, but this is worse, and it lingers. Tell me true now, girl. Do you believe a word of that tale regarding a twin brother who masquerades under his name?"

As Tiller-Parsons had suspected, they were discussing him. There had been no uncertainty in Rose's reply, though it was touched by hopelessness and despair.

"Not a word," she admitted. "I know him now for the liar he is—but what can I do? He got away with all my inheritance. It was as much from necessity as anything that I hunted him down when I happened to learn about this ranch and that he was the manager. And of course there's Alicia now. At first I was inclined to resent her, but she is just as much a victim as I am. And she's sweet. I don't want to hurt her."

"She's been hurt already; both of you have been," O'Donnell reminded her bluntly. "The man's a scoundrel. And something has to be done about it. I suppose some would say that it's none of my business, but after the way he's treated you, I'm making it mine!"

Walking, heads close together, they passed out of earshot, but Tiller-Parsons had heard enough. As he had suspected, the big cowboy was in love with his ex-wife—or whatever the relationship might be—and he had a forthright way which took no note of and gave no respect to a man's position. While as for Rose—

He'd prided himself on the adroitness with which he'd managed an almost impossible situation, but apparently he had fooled no one—perhaps not even Alicia. His two wives, thrown increasingly in each other's company, had become good friends. Perhaps they were already confiding in each other. With Rose in her present mood, they would not stop short of discussing him—

Ordinarily, he wouldn't have cared. He could find ways to keep the situation under control. But with the owners of the ranch due to arrive almost any day—

He hadn't counted on such a complication, but there was no question about it: he would have to act. Failure to do so could bring ruin. But how?

There was the rub. There were few, if any, among the ranch crew whom he could trust, particularly in so delicate a matter. The ironic part was that those on whom he could depend had been despatched with Abbott and the herd.

It would not do to be involved personally—

A tight smile did nothing to relieve the sudden cruelty at the corners of his mouth. The solution, after all, was so very simple. Moreover, he had promised Chief Spotted Pony something in return for a favor granted, and this could be made mutually profitable.

Dusk was closing over the valley like a drift of fog, blurring the outlines of the big house, masking the lesser structures. Only the savory smells of a roast of beef and of what he judged to be biscuits hot from the oven penetrated without hindrance, and O'Donnell lifted his head, swinging his eager horse toward the corrals. In that instant he heard a scream.

It came sharp yet muffled, as though choked before the sound could gasp above the throat. Simultaneously there was a quick beat of hooves, as swiftly receding.

O'Donnell was already swinging his horse, spurring. Brief and muffled though it had been, there was a quality to the voice that left no doubt in his mind. It was Rose who had cried out.

He made out the moving blur ahead as his cayuse lined out for a run, as though shadowy ghosts fled before him. The big ex-sergeant crooned in his horse's ear, stretched along its neck, and as though understanding the urgency, it lengthened its stride. So they were gaining, since one of the two horses ahead was doubly burdened, and was thus in poor condition for racing.

Now the buildings had been left behind, as they crested the slope and then lined across the easy roll of flatlands beyond. O'Donnell rode in grim silence, his mind busy with a problem. Somebody was abducting Rose, which he did not find too surprising, but who? Well, he'd get an answer.

He gave no thought to the holstered revolver at his hip. In his present mood he felt no need for more than his hands, and in any case, he couldn't chance a shot.

The space between had been halved, then

cut again. One rider turned to look back, his face only a dull blankness in the gloom. O'Donnell sensed that panic rode with the abductors. They were bunglers, not having anticipated instant pursuit; also, from the muffled grunts and exclamations, it seemed clear that Rose was far from a docile captive. Apparently she was threshing wildly, kicking, very likely using teeth and fingernails, giving her captor more than he had bargained for.

The unhindered rider suddenly swung his horse at O'Donnell's, lashing out with a tomahawk. That confirmed his guess, which had been growing into a conviction. These were Indians. But a red man could grow just as panicky as a white when things went wrong, and the frantic swing of arm and axe was easy to avoid. For a man who had more than once put his life on the line in hand-to-hand combat, it left a wide and easy opening.

Swinging close, O'Donnell closed his fingers behind the gripping hand. A violent jerk dislodged the rider and sent him flying through the night. A dismayed howl ended as suddenly as had the earlier scream, causing the sergeant to suspect that the wailer had probably gotten a mouthful of dirt.

Then he was alongside the burdened cayuse. The captive had been brought temporarily under control, held face down on the running shoulders in front of the warrior. With frantic desperation he brought up a short-barreled derringer which he had wrestled from his captive, firing at point-blank range. The flame made a crimson blossom, and O'Donnell responded, chopping with the long barrel of his own gun, raking down the skull and across the nose.

As the brave collapsed, spilling, O'Donnell snatched and caught Rose, who in turn was making a desperate if ungraceful jump toward him. Then they were together, and despite the remembered fragrance of food, O'Donnell had lost all desire to hurry.

XII

Clouds were piling to the west, a vague dark tumble suggestive of a pillow fight, while an increasing sharpness in the air betokened that the long spell of fine weather might be drawing to an end. Montana, jogging easily, driving the extra horses as he came, eyed the cluster of buildings, then another moving mass just beginning to show from the east. Swinging from almost under the gather of clouds, following the wheel trace which usage was rapidly making into a road, came a caravan of horsemen; behind them were wagons, along with a couple of two-seated carriages, then more wagons with canvas covers.

The owners of the syndicate must be arriving, Montana decided, and found the circumstances to his liking. At the same time, it was apt to bother his employer. Briefly he pondered the complications which might ensue, and his part in them. Tiller-Parsons had hired him, so technically at least he was working for him. But the Englishmen owned the outfit, paying his salary as well as that of the manager. Actually, he was working for them.

There had been plenty of time for thinking, as he followed the long trail back from the Yellowstone. He was looking forward to what might develop with considerable anticipation.

He was not supposed to return from this journey, having been marked for sacrifice. Which was but one of several matters in which the manager had interested himself, with his penchant for planning.

It was something like a rope artist displaying his skill with several lariats at one time. That always made an impressive act, as long as the performer did not become tangled in a maze of his own contriving. For a while, Montana was willing to watch the performance.

The approach of the caravan had already been noticed. Now there was a bustle of last-minute preparations at the buildings, a scurry as of hens at the shadow of a hawk. But it was an ordered haste. With a manager who planned so carefully and so far in advance, everything would be under control; everything with the exception of his own return. Tiller-Parsons would have made no plans for such an eventuality.

Tiller-Parsons came out from the big house, Alicia by his side. They had dressed for the occasion more elegantly than usual, certainly more elaborately than the natives thereabouts had ever seen. Tiller-Parsons' attitude would be correct, a nice blend of the welcoming host and the obsequious servant.

Tiller-Parsons glanced about, viewing the elegance of the fine house with conscious self-approval, certain of the good impression it must make upon his employers. From that survey he turned to see Montana swinging down from his horse.

A gambler by nature, even if somewhat lacking in the skills necessary to such a profession, Tiller-Parsons was seldom caught off guard. This time he was. Blankness, mixed with consternation, flowed across his face, and the almost colorless eyes became even lighter. He stared unbelievingly. Montana could appreciate what he felt.

Only an instant. Then Tiller-Parsons had control of himself. The mask dropped back in place, although he swallowed uncomfortably. To give him credit, he *was* a gambler, ready to put whatever fortune might be his to an instant test. Smiling, he advanced with outstretched hand.

"Montana! I was just thinking about you! You made the trip without trouble, I see?"

"No trouble at all," Montana assured him blandly, and went on to the next step, which would be at least as painful for Tiller-Parsons as his return. The housekeeper had appeared, also Rose and Tim O'Donnell, as witnesses to the transaction.

"I have the money that was paid for the cattle," Montana explained. "So I'll turn it over to you now."

He proceeded to untie a wrapped package

from behind his saddle, and for a second time, much like a fish newly pulled from the water, Tiller-Parsons swallowed. His mind worked like the frantic digging of a gopher, as a crisis closed in inexorably.

He had recognized the hazard in involving a man like Montana Abbott, who had a reputation for being able to take care of himself. But that sort of a reputation was vital in lending credibility to the loss of the money, and Tiller-Parsons hadn't seen how it could fail.

Yet fail it had, and now he was faced with a threat far more dangerous. And here was O'Donnell with Rose, smiling and polite like Abbott. What had happened to those darned Indians?

He desperately needed time to think, to deal with one thing at a time, and there was no time. His employers were arriving and must be greeted. They of course would be delighted with so early and sizable a cash dividend from the ranch operations. The painful part was having the money in his hands, but with no chance to hang onto it. He managed a desperate sort of calmness.

"Excellent, Abbott," he agreed. "I'm delighted, of course—both at how you've managed and at your safe return. Right now our employers are arriving."

It was a temporary relief to be able to turn as the buggies came up and began to disgorge their passengers. A driver was in each, leaving six seats for the guests of honor. His glance ranged quickly. Sir John and Lady Crispin, the former as red-faced and hearty as his lady was thin and ascetic in appearance—one did not apply the adjective vinegary to a woman of such distinction—

Mr. Silvanus Drew, sagging the buggy step and spring, backing out and down as ponderously as a hog for the weighing—Tiller-Parsons' mind recoiled with a start from the comparison, however apt—

The Right Honorable Thomas Noonan, M. P., and Mrs. Noonan, both looking precisely and exactly right, even at the end of so long and wearing a journey—

Tiller-Parsons lost color, gulping a third time. Mr. Byron Fancher, manager of the company as well as the syndicate—and Tiller-Parsons understood that much more than this Montana ranch was involved—Fancher should have been the sixth notable. Instead, he was dismounting, a shade stiffly but with a suggestion of sprightliness, from a horse, while the other passenger—

The pale eyes seemed to recede, blinking rapidly. This was a nightmare, dynamite and disaster. It was as startling and impossible as finding Rose here at the ranch, when he had arrived with Alicia as his bride. Somehow he had weathered that, even though his solution now seemed in danger of falling apart. But this—

However overweight and ponderous of manner, Mr. Silvanus Drew was reported to be a friend of the Prince. He was one of the manner born, doubly fortunate in being the possessor of a more than ample fortune. He was dressed as he deemed the occasion merited, in boots and rough tweeds topped by a real cowboy hat. Despite his bulk, he looked and felt at home, turning from assisting the final passenger down from the double-seater. His smile was warm as it rested upon Tiller-Parsons—deceptively so, the latter suspected, and could think only of the satisfied, wide-toothed grin of a well-fed wolf.

The lady on Drew's arm was slender, smartly dressed, and as strikingly beautiful in her way as Rose or Alicia, a pale-gold blondeness suggestive of silver and gold. She was painfully familiar to Tiller-Parsons, and Mr. Drew was presenting her, with the air of a man who delighted in happy surprises.

"Look whom I ran across in London, just the week before we sailed, and brought along to make the party complete," he said. "A happy surprise, eh, old boy? Mrs. Jennifer Tiller-Parsons herself!"

It seemed to Tiller-Parsons, gasping again after the manner of a fish, that these low blows were coming unduly thick and fast. For an instant, panic gripped him. But having been through this before, experience steadied him. He drew back a pace, and by then his mind commenced to work again.

"I'm delighted to see you again, sir—all of you. But is this some sort of a spoof? Yet I'm only too afraid that I understand," he added grimly.

"Spoof? Understand?" The solidity of Drew was thoroughly British. "What do you mean? You should be overjoyed to see your wife again."

Everyone was staring, all else held in abeyance, with varying interest and anticipation. Tiller-Parsons' shake of the head was resigned, almost forgiving.

"As it happens, Mr. Drew, I have a wife—but only one," he added. "To my regret, I also have a twin brother, who for reasons of his own, unknown to me, appears to have assumed my name and identity—in a deception of which this lady seems to have been the most recent victim."

Jennifer was eying him with incredulity and anger. She was slightly smaller than the other ladies of his choice, but vibrant now as a too tight fiddle string. Eyes normally violet but now almost black swept him furiously.

"So to top all the rest, you lie about it now?" she demanded. "With you, I'm past being surprised."

"There you differ from me, madam." Tiller-Parsons contrived a sweeping bow. "These surprises still startle me. I only wish that they did not discommode such charming and lovely ladies!"

Montana had to admire his adroitness. The man was a scoundrel; of that he had received more than enough proof. On the broad pattern, he was also a skillful planner, but he was like an overly busy spider in a high wind, weaving so many webs that he was getting entangled in them.

But his alibi had worked once, and it was equally convincing now. If his twin brother had deserted Rose as soon as he had gotten his hands on her money, why should he not use the same formula a second time? It seemed clear that he had taken ship for England, to be well away from Rose. With an ocean between, and his charm for the ladies undiminished, he had considered it safe to marry Jennifer.

As the supposed facts were gradually brought to light, Jennifer regarded the other ladies appraisingly. Then she made a confession which a lady to the manner born might have found humiliating.

"So he rooked you, did he?" she demanded of Rose. "The same with me, I'm afraid. Fifteen thousand pounds, the stinkin' blighter! Told me he had a chance to myke a fortune, off here in America—and myde me believe it! Then he walked out on me—not realizing that I had as much more left!"

She swung suddenly to Alicia, who during the interchange had been a silent onlooker.

"And how much has he rooked you for? For with him, it's just a gyme to steal. That's all he ever wants from any of us is our money!"

Alicia caught Tiller-Parsons' appealing glance, but her own was as considering as it was troubled.

"There was a matter of some forty thousand dollars," she admitted. "These twins seem to have certain traits in common."

"Oh, now, my dear!" Tiller-Parsons' protest was pained.

Alicia's rejoinder was even more devastating.

"Perhaps we might form a club," she suggested brightly. "There are enough of us. We could call ourselves The Cast-offs."

XIII

There was spitefulness in the remark, but Montana sensed the deep underlying hurt. Along with that, there was the hurt which had not quite been laid to rest with his initial explanation, and now was sharpened almost to conviction. It was the deadly parallel, the wheedling of huge sums of money from each bride, which did it. Had that been an attribute only of the supposed twin, not touching Tiller-Parsons, his alibi would have been acceptable.

Still, it was an alibi, and Tiller-Parsons clung to it with the stubbornness of desperation. The homecoming of the owners of the ranch was marred but not quite spoiled, and one factor on which Tiller-Parsons had failed to count in all his careful planning went a long way to balance the scales in his favor. That was the cash profit, the sizable dividend realized on the sale of the herd, which he was able to present to them.

Nor did he weaken his case by any reference to what his graceless brother might have done with such a sum of money.

Montana might have tipped the scales by telling what he knew or suspected, but that was between the two of them; he owed a certain loyalty to the outfit if not to Tiller-Parsons, and there already was uproar enough. For the present, he would wait.

On the surface it appeared an uneasy draw, with none of those involved quite believing Tiller-Parsons, yet not entirely doubting him. With a half-guilty sense for the fitness of things, each one attempted to restore pleasant relations, with at least outward success.

Tiller-Parsons did not delude himself into any such belief. This had been an incredible chain of events, resulting in all three of his wives turning up on this ranch, and he was still bewildered by the sequence. When he had left Rose, taking ship for England, he had counted the episode as over and done with, to his own profit. Certainly she was a lovely lady, who had believed his protestations, but a man on the make could not afford to let sentiment stand in his way.

That she might one day read in a newspaper feature about an English syndicate which had acquired a Montana ranch and employed him to manage it—or that she would or could make her way to that ranch, he would have dismissed as unthinkable.

Similarly, it had seemed a perfect opportunity to repeat the already successful formula by marrying an English girl who was charmed as much by his supposed social position as by himself. Since she would be not merely disappointed but furious at his inability to make good, it had been best conveniently to lose her, by again boarding a ship for the States.

Even should she discover that much, she would look for him along the Eastern seaboard, rather than across a continent. The odd chance that she might somewhere have made the acquaintance of one of the owners of the ranch had certainly never occurred to him.

It had been a long day, and tiring. Tiller-Parsons winced as pain racked his shoulder, a short quick stab, as swiftly gone. A knife had cut there years before, twisting and gouging, and though the wound had long since healed, he suffered an occasional reminder. Now his mouth twisted. That fracas had been over a woman.

Soberly, he took stock of the day's events. They had been unpleasant, but he was sure that he had put on a convincing show. And in a way, it made sense.

"I'd almost have liked to know you," he paid tribute to his mythical twin. "There's no doubt that you're a scoundrel of the first water; still in all, you're a man after my own heart!"

With all three of his wives thrown together at the ranch, the next few days would be risky. He would have to tread warily. Even his encounter with the drink-sodden chief had hardly been more precarious. It would take only a single miscue to render his position untenable.

A very present danger was Montana Abbott. He too, had a fund of knowledge which he'd be pondering, and sooner or later, he would demand an accounting. It was not a reckoning to look forward to.

Then, like a ripple of heat lightning along a distant horizon, the solution came to him. Tiller-Parsons stared at the darkness and shook his head, appalled at the fertility of his imagination. It could be a complete and final way of solving his problems, all of them, and with little or no risk.

But he wasn't a savage—at least not yet. Angrily he rejected the thought, which had come unbidden, frighteningly.

He had managed to slip away, to stroll by himself, to settle his shaken nerves and ponder. This early in the evening, although it was late in the fall, the air was almost balmy. Somewhere, from the hilltop back of the buildings, a coyote's cry quavered, rising, hanging on a note of mockery.

Still, taking the idea on a reduced scale, it might present a solution. Actually, something of the sort would be no worse than what he had already intended to set for Abbott, a trap which he had somehow eluded.

It was time to be getting back to Alicia, to make sure that, despite her comment in which hurt had wailed, she was not too disturbed by the accusations. Somehow, to gain time, he must contrive to keep the three women from getting together and comparing notes. He must be especially nice to all three, each in the right fashion. Also, there would have to be some entertainment provided for his visitors, something to keep everyone occupied. That was it. Appeal to Alicia, as his wife—to her sense of duty as the hostess, let her know how much he needed and depended on her. The planning for the entertainment of their guests would give her something to do—

He was startled to find their room empty. It had been too much to hope that he might find Alicia asleep, despite the lateness of the hour. The day's events had been too disturbing for sleep to come easily, and she would probably have a lot of questions.

Not only was the room empty, but her clothes were gone. Tiller-Parsons was suddenly uneasy at what that implied.

The housekeeper was still up, busy with numerous duties because of the influx of guests. He caught the gleam of a lamp as she moved along a hallway and hurried to question her.

"Do you know where my wife has gone?" he asked uneasily. "She isn't in our room—"

The normally pleasant face behind the high-held lamp was rigid and unfriendly.

"If you mean Miss Alicia, she moved to the empty room at the far end of the upper hall," was the retort, and lady and lamp receded along the passage in an aura of disapproval.

Shaking his head, Tiller-Parsons stared after her. It looked as though all the ladies were badly ruffled and were taking a stand against him. Yet how could a man have foreseen such events as had come to pass? After all of his contriving, it was incredible.

Alicia opened the door at his knock, but her eyes were cool and unfriendly. He pushed past her and closed the door.

"What is the meaning of this, my dear?" he asked, and realized how inane the question was. "Surely you don't believe those wild accusations? We've been over all of that before—"

"I thought, under the circumstances, that it would be better if I was off here by myself," Alicia returned. "Better for everyone."

"But that's ridiculous," he protested. "You're my wife. *They* married my twin brother—"

Her look checked him. She was smiling, her lips tired and wistful, but edged with scorn.

"Did they?" she countered. "It won't wash, my friend. It was a good try, but too far-fetched."

"Far-fetched?" he repeated, suddenly desperate. "But it's the truth. You've got to believe me—"

"You see," she went on, as though not hearing, "we compared notes, the three of us. It was Jennifer who thought of your scar."

"Scar?" Tiller-Parsons repeated stupidly. "But I have no scar—"

"Oh, but you do, Lothario. I suppose you never get to see it, and perhaps didn't even know about it. But it's on your left shoulder, on your back, just out of sight. A sort of white blotch, as though it had been made by a knife. All three of us have seen it. And it would be odd indeed for you and a twin each to have received a wound which would cause such a scar in exactly the same place."

With final cold deliberation, she shut the door in his face.

XIV

Tiller-Parsons stared blankly at the closed door, his mind equally shut. Here was disaster, complete and final. As he stumbled out into the night, he had no doubts on that score. He was undone, past all explaining—all on account of a scar which he had never seen or suspected.

The Englishmen, once the truth was known, would be horrified and outraged. His career in their employ would be summarily ended.

The worst of it was that losing his job would be only the start. Their suspicions having been aroused on one point, Mr. Gates, the manager, would be certain to start investigating, to dig into other aspects, such as his expenditures—

The moon was up, the evening still balmy. Tiller-Parsons brought up abruptly as he encountered another stroller. As though his thinking had conjured him up, Horatio Gates hailed him affably, removing a pipe from his mouth to gesture toward the moon.

"Ah there, Tiller-Parsons. A beautiful evening."

"Is it? I hadn't noticed."

"I suppose all this is an old story to you—the grandeur of the scenery, the wide sweep of plain and prairie, the mountains against the skyline. To me, it is all new and entrancing. I am certainly impressed. What you have accomplished here, sir, is outstanding."

"I'm happy that you approve—"

"Oh, I do, sir, I do, though in all honesty, there are certain aspects of the overall picture, certain matters which I do not fully understand. Probably it is on that account, because of an incomplete picture, that I find them disturbing. Perhaps you can enlighten me."

Here it is, Tiller-Parsons thought grimly. Lying would be of no further use, since all three of the women he had married had made up their minds. Turning, Gates climbed with surprising nimbleness to perch on a top pole of the corral, so there was nothing to do but take a seat beside him. Unhurriedly, the general manager knocked out his pipe against the log, then tucked it carefully away in a pouch.

"We were several days on the road, down from the river at Fort Benton," he explained precisely. "A most interesting journey, but that is beside the point. What I have in mind was an encounter, a couple of days ago, with a sick man. Badly injured would perhaps be a more accurate description, since his fever and sickness derived from a festering wound. It had been caused by an arrow—an Indian arrow, he told me. It struck me as little short of a miracle that he had not only survived such a wound, but had traveled a considerable distance on foot before being found by us."

Puzzled, Tiller-Parsons listened.

"I'm afraid I don't grasp your point," he confessed.

"Probably not. We did what we could for the fellow, giving him a horse and other needed supplies, after which he went on, being quite insistent on that point. He seemed very anxious to get away from that country once and for all. That became understandable, once he recounted the harrowing experiences he had undergone."

And I'm in about the same boat, Tiller-Parsons reflected, his apprehensions increasing.

"He poured a strange and, at times, unbelievable tale into my ears," Gates went on. "It seems that he had been taking a wagonload of liquor to the Indians—an undertaking which I understand is forbidden, as well as hazardous. I presume he hoped to sell or trade the goods for a fancy price, but matters didn't work out. The Indians helped themselves, without pay, and he was lucky to escape with his life, though receiving a wound from an arrow. Understandably, he wanted nothing more to do with them."

"I shouldn't think he would."

"Indeed he did not." Gates peered placidly at the moon, which gave the appearance of wearing a halo. Tiller-Parsons guessed that the ring was a portent of bad weather on the way, putting an end to the fine fall, and he viewed it with distaste. It was uncomfortably like an omen.

"The background to this trader's activities was what most interested me," Gates went on. "Perhaps he was imagining certain matters, or it may have been the effect of the fever. On the whole, however, he seemed rational, as well as very much in earnest. He claimed to have been one of a crew of cattle drovers—cowboys, I presume is the correct term—escorting a trail herd up from Texas. Somewhere in the Wind River country, wherever that is, he described how they were set upon—not by red men but by white.

"Apparently it was rather awful, a bloody butchery. Massacre was the word he used, he being one of the few to escape alive. And the cattle were stolen—rustled was his term."

A light wind had sprung up, bringing a sudden chill, but Tiller-Parsons found himself sweating. He waited grimly.

"It was this man's contention that the herd was thus obtained by its new owners not alone by fraud, but by murder and treachery. He insisted further—and this I find the next unbelievable part of his tale—that the Powder River Ranch received this herd. His own subsequent activities, as he explained them, were prompted by a desire to see justice done, to avenge his fallen comrades."

Gates' voice was calm and without expression, but he had stated his case and posed a question. Tiller-Parsons' earlier guess, that he had deliberately chosen some subject far afield, thus tactfully avoiding reference to Tiller-Parsons' domestic troubles, had been wide of the mark. To the manager's mind, this was connected, but far more serious. And he was a man who would insist on a full and believable answer.

"I had heard of the man you mention and his suspicions," Hank acknowledged. "I've tried to verify them—so far without much success. The crew who delivered the herd here carried the proper papers regarding the stock, so the transaction was concluded according to arrangements already made. If they were the wrong crew, and guilty of such an act, I had no reason to suspect them at the time. Tomorrow I'll show you the records, and we'll go into this in greater detail."

"Of course, of course," Gates agreed. "I'm sure that you're as anxious to get at the truth of this as I am. Meanwhile, we'll say nothing to the others, to spoil their pleasure in this journey. And I'm afraid I'm keeping you from your rest."

With a cheerful good night, he climbed down and disappeared within the big house. Tiller-Parsons remained seated, staring unseeingly at the moon. He had already given all the explanation he could, and all at once, nothing that he said was being accepted.

What should be his next move? A woman scorned was bad enough—but three of them, now leagued together—

He might steal away in the night, fleeing ignominiously. That would mean ruin, and even the frontier would not be wide enough. Still worse, to run would be a highly dangerous undertaking. If he blundered into Indians, any Indians, they would kill him. If he was lucky enough to evade them, there would still be pursuit, for many potent causes. A tracker as skilled as Montana

Abbott would probably run him to earth within a matter of hours, certainly of days.

The earlier solution was suddenly impelling, insistent. He stared into the darkness, appalled. Whatever he had intended, when setting out on this planned trail to success, he had not contemplated murder or massacre—

But there had been robbery, bigamy, wife desertion, along with a host of lesser offenses. And traceable to him, the accusations almost leveled, were murder and massacre—

Dropping to the ground, he began a restless pacing, sweating, rejecting notions as they flocked. Only one of them appeared to be workable, to be certain in its effect. His mind kept reverting to it as would a gopher to its burrow. As with the rodent, when a fox prowled in the brush and a hawk sailed overhead, there was nowhere else to go.

And after all, why not? These others, all of them, were already thirsting for *his* blood, not literally but in ways almost equally unpleasant. It had become either him or them. With events driving him on, he was left no other choice.

The scheme, as he pondered it, seemed almost flawless. This was the frontier, remote and beyond the law. The Indians were restless, friendly on the surface, yet guilty of isolated outrages. The guilt for what occurred would fall, as it should, upon them—and there would be no one to contradict, nor even to dispute what had happened.

Spotted Pony would prove a ready and willing instrument, for a number of reasons. He could sack the ranch, and it would yield a huge booty, just as a massacre would jibe with his desires.

It would be days, or more likely weeks, before anyone would know what had happened. With the land buried under winter snows, some might suspect where the guilt lay, but there would be no proof, nothing to connect any single band with the outrage.

There would be no survivors. That was regrettable, but again the necessities of his own survival dictated how it must be. The Indians would see it the same way.

He would be counted as one of the dead. Not alone this chapter, but the book would be closed. Somewhere else, under a new name and identity, he would start anew. And with a little luck, he would be able to salvage enough for an excellent start.

Tiller-Parsons sighed, but the sharpness of his regret was already dulled. This had been forced upon him, and it was the only possible decision. A man could do no less.

The immediate problem was how to get word to Spotted Pony, to arrange a meeting. It would have to be secret, and whoever carried word had to be reasonably trustworthy, as well as skilled enough in the ways of the country to manage, without losing his own hair in the doing.

Being short-handed as far as trustworthy members of the ranch crew were concerned posed a problem. When he had sent those others off with Montana and the herd, he had not foreseen such a contingency.

In his mind he reviewed everyone who might be available. He fixed on one of the men who had come in that day with the new arrivals. Dutch Cassidy should do very well.

Tiller-Parsons did not know a geat deal about him, but enough. Cassidy belonged to that drifting army of homeless men who prowled the land like lost souls. He had known Bannack and Virginia City in the heyday of the Innocents. He had run the rivers, trapping, prospecting, scouting, freighting. He was passable at most tasks, not very good at any.

One thing he had in common with most

of that faceless legion. For a price, usually not a very high one, he would do anything.

Returning to the house, moving with stealthy quietness, Tiller-Parsons found paper, a quill and ink. Not risking a candle, he wrote by the light of the moon. Only a few words were necessary, to whet the chief's curiosity and arrange a meeting. Spotted Pony could read English writing as well as he spoke the language.

In the meanwhile, Tiller-Parsons decided, while the details were being worked out, he would ignore the unpleasantries of the day and arrange some sort of entertainment for the newcomers. It was essential to preserve at least a surface amity, to keep them happy. And as manager for the ranch, that was his job.

XV

Because Tiller-Parsons was at some pains to make it sound like an innocent, routine job, Dutch Cassidy knew that it must be something other than that. But the ranch foreman—Cassidy did not distinguish between the two managers—was paying him well for the task, and in advance. What his particular business might be, Cassidy accounted as none of his affair.

He had second thoughts upon learning that the message was to be delivered to an Indian.

"That makes no danger for you," Tiller-Parsons reassured him. "I know that some of the redskins are restless, but you will wear a white hat. That will assure you safe conduct with Spotted Pony and his band."

"I don't have any white hat," Cassidy reminded him dubiously, but Tiller-Parsons provided one. Clearly all this means for communication had been planned in advance.

Simply to deliver a message had sounded reasonable enough as he rode out from the ranch buildings. Out of sight of them and alone in the night, Cassidy's doubts flooded back. Removing the hat and holding it close in front of his eyes, now that the moon had dipped below the horizon, he could barely make out a vague blur. If some trigger-happy warrior should choose to shoot, instead of waiting to get a close look—

But trouble, when it came, was from a source he had not expected. Another rider loomed in the night, offering a challenge. Cassidy was both relieved and disturbed as he recognized Montana's voice.

"You'll have some reason for riding abroad at such an hour, I'm sure," Montana suggested. "I'm curious as to what it is."

Unable to think of a convincing lie, Cassidy fell back on the truth. After all, he had been given no directions to the contrary. Montana listened and nodded agreeably.

"You're to deliver a note to Chief Spotted Pony himself," he repeated. "All right. There's just one thing. Let me know what he says or does after you've delivered it."

"I'll do that," Cassidy agreed, reflecting that he would let circumstances decide. Riding on, and having been mindful on the journey to the ranch where the Indians almost certainly lurked, he was able to deliver the letter to Spotted Pony. The braves who intercepted him had noted the hat and been not unfriendly.

The chief read the missive and grunted. His next reaction, Cassidy found less to his liking.

"I will meet him tomorrow night," Spotted Pony agreed. "But to make sure that there is no double-cross, you will remain here, at this camp, until I ride to meet him. When I go, you can go also."

It occurred to Cassidy, considering all that

he had heard at the ranch and here, that there was no love lost between a lot of different people; certainly there was no trust. But he was treated well enough, spending most of the day sleeping. The difficulty was that both Tiller-Parsons and Montana might be put out at his failure to report back, but that could not be helped.

One thing he could do, he decided, once he was permitted to set out, along with Spotted Pony. At the moment, sided by shadows, the darkness was heavy. Cassidy allowed his horse to drop back; then he was alone.

He was faced with a choice, one of three possibilities. He might return straight to the ranch, or make the most of the opportunity to get out of the country. Or he could spy on the meeting between Spotted Pony and Tiller-Parsons. He had learned where the rendezvous was to take place.

That might be a chancy business, but he swung and headed for the spot. By now, their meeting appeared far less casual and innocent than he had first supposed.

Almost certainly it was none of his business, a fact he'd do well to keep in mind. The trouble, Dutch decided with a resigned sigh, was that he was just lacking in good sense. Or perhaps he was overly curious.

He almost blundered. Tiller-Parsons had named Bald Rock as the place for the meeting, and Cassidy, misjudging landmarks in the darkness, assumed that he had some distance yet to go. Voices just ahead brought him up short; then he leaned forward in the saddle, ears attuned to listen.

The two men were arguing, not amicably. Tiller-Parsons' nerves had been worn raw by recent events, and he felt that he was offering a favor, but the chief seemed to believe that it was the other way around. Both had grown angry. Cassidy's blood chilled at the chief's words.

"You said, let us understand each other," Spotted Pony said in measured tones. "I understand you very well. There are certain ones on your ranch who are in your way, and you want them out of the way. But instead of doing your own killing, you want me to do the dirty work. Very well. I will do so. But when my braves attack, we will make a clean sweep, killing everyone. Doing it that way will be much better for both of us. No one will remain alive to ask questions or to answer them."

"But I don't want a massacre," Tiller-

Parsons protested. His qualms still bothered him. "If you can take some scalps and loot the place—"

Spotted Pony checked him impatiently. Along with hatred for the white man in general, he had acquired an overriding contempt for this one in particular.

"It will be done my way," he declared. "That is the only safe method for both of us. Now as to the time—"

Tiller-Parsons gave in, not too reluctantly. It dawned on him that the chief was not only ready to cooperate and enthusiastic, but that he had exhibited no surprise at the proposition. *He's been planning such an attack. I'm only making it easier for him.*

The certainty that Spotted Pony would have struck in any case eased his scruples. He could hardly be counted as responsible.

He might, of course, return and warn the others, in a new twist to the double-cross, but that would be as foolish as it would be useless. They could not escape by running, nor were they in sufficient force to make a successful stand against attack.

The only result would be to get himself killed without helping the others. As it was, he and Spotted Pony were each doing the other a favor.

That was the comfortable as well as the sensible way to look at matters; still, he was a bit staggered to find himself not merely a party to so murderous a scheme, but a prime mover in it. He was most shaken at the realization that he was relieved rather than otherwise, because the chief insisted on doing a complete job.

Where the visiting Englishmen were concerned, it was most regrettable. But it was their misfortune to have arrived at so inopportune a time, without consulting him in advance. He could have warned them that the natives were restless.

Riding, absorbed in his thoughts, Tiller-Parsons heard nothing of the commotion behind.

Having pulled up at a convenient vantage point, Dutch Cassidy listened to the argument with increasing shock and disbelief. The two chiefs, who differed only in the color of their skins, were discussing details of a massacre as casually as though it were no more than a hunt for buffalo. Having heard of Spotted Pony, Cassidy could understand the Indian's point of view. His was an implacable hatred for all whites, and he was being offered a perfect chance for revenge. It was hardly to be expected that he would do otherwise than accept.

But Tiller-Parsons was supposedly of a different ilk. Occupying a responsible position, and accepted on terms of equality by the Englishmen, he was callously betraying them, merely because he faced ruin if they remained on the scene. Dutch Cassidy made no pretensions to idealism, but he was appalled at the deal.

It was a deal in which he, along with all the others, was scheduled to die.

Having been used as a go-between or messenger made it worse. Some of the responsibility was being foisted on him.

There was no time to think or plan, but in Dutch's case there was no need to do either. He knew what he must do, what he would do. He would get back and reveal the plot to Montana, as he had been asked to; after that, it would be Montana's responsibility.

What they might do then, beyond putting up a fight and going down honorably instead of being murdered without warning, Cassidy could not imagine. He was forced to an acceptance of the conclusion which he had just heard advanced: that the odds against them would be overwhelming. But it was better to fight.

Also, he'd heard that Montana Abbott had been an army officer, a leader of forlorn causes. He might come up with something—

Automatically, with a reflex action, he jerked his horse to a stop. Why leave it to Montana, the whole matter to an increasingly uncertain future, when he could handle it himself, quickly and easily?

More bewildered than astonished at the inspiration, Dutch shook his head at the audacity of the idea. Out of nowhere, it had popped into his head. He could kill the chief!

If he did that, with no one around to hear or know, it would certainly have some effect on events and their outcome. It would be some hours before the dead man was found, and once the warriors discovered him, there would be confusion. They would, of course, be out for revenge, but leaderless, lacking any particular plan. That would give Montana a better chance to counter the attack. In any case, the situation could hardly be worsened.

Cassidy swung his horse, then spurred. He was accustomed to obeying orders, not initiating action, but this was simple and direct enough for anyone, and there was no time to lose.

Spotted Pony was a dim blur in the night, a receding splotch in the darkness. He'd have to get closer, to make sure—

Cassidy was leaning forward, leveling his gun, his horse at a run. Half-consciously he was aware that this was rougher country than he'd been traversing before, when suddenly the other horseman swung about. Spotted Pony had heard the pursuit, of course, and he was ready to fight—

The two guns blasted almost as one, small crimson blossoms against the vastness of the dark. It came to Dutch Cassidy that he had been a trifle slow, not capitalizing on the advantage or the initial surprise that had been his.

Whether his own bullet sped wild or was accurate, he had no idea, but the Indian was either lucky or a marksman; confusedly, Cassidy remembered having heard that Spotted Pony had been trained in the white man's ways.

His horse was hit; the slogging, staggering impact of the heavy-caliber bullet seemed to rock Cassidy as well as the animal. It almost halted the running cayuse in midstride. Then, with a frantic leap of reaction, the pony was off the trail, soaring into space, falling, tumbling—taking him with it to oblivion.

There was no time to think, no chance to help himself. If it was true that in such a critical instant one remembered the events of a lifetime, apparently he did not fit the pattern. He had time for a single thought: this particular section of country was a lot rougher than he'd supposed, and he had no doubt that the drop he was taking, along with his horse, would finish what the bullet had begun.

A solid, heavy crunch, remorseless as a grinding boot, testified that they had hit, but the jarring impact was not final. The dead horse was still tumbling, but he and the cayuse had parted company, both going down, with even blacker depths below.

He hit again, and this time it was a springing yet savage thing, a lashing of tree branches as they yielded to the impact, bending, tossing him off again. Far from gentle though it was, the bounce broke his straight fall. He hit again, shockingly, the breath driven from his body. Other sounds, still drifting upward, no longer troubled his ears.

XVI

A trifle belatedly, Tiller-Parsons was making discoveries about women in general and the trio he had led to the altar in particular. Courted and cherished, they could be as lovely as a dream. Tricked and deserted, they could reveal steel beneath the softness.

Jennifer Jones, as Tiller-Parsons had discovered during the period of their courtship, was of a saucy disposition, as pert as a jay-bird. At first this trait had delighted him. Had it been profitable really to love a woman, he felt that she might easily have been the one.

Accosting him brightly, she surveyed him, head tilted to one side, much as she might consider the good points of a horse. Under the scrutiny, Tiller-Parsons refrained with difficulty from squirming.

"It's a strange coincidence," she murmured. "On the day that I met you, I had been reading a novel dealing with ancient

Chinese customs. The heroine of the tale was the number two wife."

Tiller-Parsons' somewhat desperate search for an apt rejoinder failed. Jennifer went on with a laugh, as though all this were vastly amusing.

"I never dreamed that I was slated for the same role." She smiled. "But I suppose you were following the old adage: that there is safety in numbers. Isn't it a pity that it doesn't hold good? Almost as much as that so many of us should have been so deceived by your passionate protestations! But at least we have each of us learned *our* lesson. So we intend, all for your own good of course, dear sir, to make sure that *you* learn your lesson!"

Tiller-Parsons' career had hinged on a glib tongue. Now it failed him.

"The three of us have talked things over, Henry, and have decided to give you a reprieve," Jennifer went on; "not because you deserve it, or even because we have any inclination to show you mercy. It's simply a matter of courtesy, of hospitality. Our hosts have invested a lot of money in this ranching enterprise. You have made sure of that. They have come a long way to see the country and enjoy a vacation, so on our part, it seems only fair to make their stay as enjoyable as possible.

"Because of them, Henry, we're declaring a truce for an indefinite time. Its duration will depend on your behavior. We are ready to do our best to make it an enjoyable occasion for everyone."

"That—that's very considerate of you," Tiller-Parsons stammered.

"We think so," Jennifer assured him sweetly.

Relieved, Tiller-Parsons was glibly voluble. Jennifer listened to his promises with a smile; still, he was certain that his charm was as potent as in the past. Men might dislike and distrust him, but that seemed only to enhance his appeal to the ladies.

"This is very good of you," he added. "And I'll do my best. As soon as I learned that our guests were on the way, I started to plan for their entertainment. Alicia and I discussed the possibilities and hit upon something in the nature of a housewarming. Some of the cowboys are musically inclined with such instruments as banjo and fiddle. We can invite the neighbors and have a dance. I'm afraid it won't quite equal an old-fashioned English ball, but it should be enjoyable."

Jennifer eyed him in amazement.

"A ball?" she repeated. "Here? But where are these neighbors of whom you speak so lightly?"

He waved a vague hand.

"A couple of ranches are within riding distance, and they'll be glad to come. Entertainments are all too rare here on the frontier. I'm going to leave the details up to you and the others. If you will take charge, I'm sure it will prove a memorable occasion."

Jennifer eyed him suspiciously. He was almost too agreeable. But she had made the suggestion, and it would give everyone a part, all working together. The ball was discussed with their hosts, who were also the guests; then everyone set to work making preparations.

Tiller-Parsons watched, hiding a sardonic smile. This dance or housewarming would be a climax to the visit, and it should prove a memorable one, even if not quite what they expected. Having been reasonably certain that everyone would cooperate, purely as a matter of good breeding, he had anticipated the event, conditioning his planning and Spotted Pony's upon it.

Watching the preparations, he knew a qualm of regret. The thing was rather less than sportsmanlike, to say the least, and Spotted Pony's warriors would be merciless. But the intentions of all these others, over the long run and in regard to him, left him no choice. And if the climax did not come at the ball, it would be just as savage and final, wherever it was played out. Spotted Pony had waited a long while for such a chance, and he could not be deterred or swayed from it, even if Tiller-Parsons should be so foolish as to beg him on his knees.

Self-interest demanded that he work with the Indians. Everyone, from Jennifer to Horatio Gates, had made it plain that this interlude would be followed by an accounting. That would spell ruin, and it had to be forestalled, no matter what the cost.

On the surface, a light-hearted gaiety prevailed, but to Montana, aware of the undercurrents and all that was held in abeyance, it was like the lull in the eye of a hurricane. To find himself in the hurricane's eye was not a new experience. He had known it literally during the war, caught with his command on the coast and far to the south, when a storm had swept up from the gulf with devastating effect. The momentary lull near the middle of the onslaught had been less a reprieve than a warning of worse to come.

He had the same feeling now. Contests were temporarily in abeyance, as the oil of civilization was interposed between abrasive forces. But this surface politeness only meant a delay, though he hoped that amicable solutions might be reached because of the breathing space.

As he worked with the others, to decorate the house and grounds, there was almost a festive air. Everyone took part, Paper chains were strung, after the manner which Montana remembered as a small boy at Christmas, but more elaborately. A myriad of ornaments came magically into being. There was a breathless quality to the excitement, the anticipation of women, which communicated itself, along with their loveliness.

They almost managed to make-believe, to cover the hurt each had received. The trouble was that he had felt the power of the hurricane and worked with a grim awareness that the lull would be temporary.

Horatio Gates came to him with an innocent-sounding question.

"Have you seen Dutch Cassidy?" he asked. "He's a cowboy, who made the journey here with us from the river. I can't seem to find him anywhere."

It might be that Tiller-Parsons had sent him with an invitation to one of the other ranches. Montana sought him out to inquire. From the vantage point of a ladder, as he held a paper chain near the ceiling of the big parlor, Tiller-Parsons shook his head.

"I'm sure I wouldn't know about him," he denied. "I've scarcely met him, actually."

That seemed reasonable, so Montana was inclined to accept the assertion at face value. But Timothy O'Donnell, whom he questioned next, was more helpful, while at the same time stirring doubt.

"Yeah, he's gone," he confirmed. "I don't know where or what he had in mind, but I saw him take off last night. Likely Tiller-Parsons can tell you."

"I just talked with him, and he claims not to know anything about Cassidy."

"Then he's lying. Cassidy had been powwowin' with him, so I figured Tiller-Parsons had given him some orders. Ain't seen Cassidy since."

"You're sure it was Cassidy that you saw? It couldn't have been someone else?"

"It could have been, only it wasn't. The

two of us had been chewin' the fat earlier in the evenin'. Turned out, when he got to comparin' notes, that my folks and his had both come from the same part of Ireland, on the Shannon. Both of them sailed the same year. We kind of hit it off together, Dutch and me. We was aimin' to visit some more today."

Montana's nod was grim. Here it was again, and the unreasonable quality of Tiller-Parsons' denial was like a stone in a shoe. Why should he lie about such a matter, when there seemed no reason for it? But Montana was certain that Tiller-Parsons never did anything without a reason.

As ranch manager, he had worked hard today, entering in the spirit of the occasion, laughing and joking, managing to provide almost everything that the ladies required. He had made himself so agreeable that almost everyone seemed inclined to be more lenient, if not forgiving . . . .

"I think I'll take a look around for Cassidy," Montana decided. "Keep an eye on things till I get back."

O'Donnell nodded.

"That I will," he agreed. "But it's not me that needs to be observant. If you'll pardon my saying so, Captain, somebody's mighty busy tryin' to pull the wool over our eyes. All this stuff that we're doing keeps everybody busy, not leavin' too much time to think about other matters. But I don't like none of it. Be careful as you ride, man!"

XVII

Dutch Cassidy was slow in returning to consciousness, a circumstance to be wondered at only in that he might not have been expected to regain it at all. He endured a dark period of transition, which lasted through the remaining hours of the night. During that time he hovered like a startled bird between life and death, the possibility of sudden flight uncomfortably balanced.

When finally his eyes opened, to stare at first on vacancy, his mind was as slow and clogged as the hoofs of a horse plodding through deep, clinging mud. To shake off the feeling of lethargy which held him and rouse himself was a weary process.

But gradually the unending drum of pain, hammering against the roof of his skull, became bearable. His eyes focused, and individual aches and pains began to sort themselves out into an intolerable list. They seemed everywhere, through all his body, and it was only as he was able to remember that he understood.

There had been the plunging fall of his stricken horse, dropping into black depths at the side. He had been bounced from the saddle as the horse struck and bounced also in the descent. That might account for the effects which he was now feeling. What really surprised him was being able to feel, to be alive.

That had happened during the night. Now it was daylight; the sun was shifting to shine against his face. Moving to avoid it, stiffly and painfully, he shrank in sudden terror, striving to draw back, finding himself staring over the side into those black depths which he had almost supposed to be part of a nightmare.

Pulling back, gasping, he took stock. He was sprawled on solid rock, and a ledge of smooth, dark rock rose up behind him. On the other side, an equally sheer wall fell away to the depths. The ledge on which he lay was less than half a dozen feet in width, and to already bruised bones and flesh it was intolerably unyielding.

How far the ledge might run, in either direction, he had no idea.

Risking another look, he saw that the canyon at the side was deep, though not very wide. The opposite wall was almost within jumping distance, had he been in shape to leap or had any reason to do so. Both walls of the canyon reared upward. On the opposite side, only a little higher up, a pine tree had found a precarious hold.

Existence for the tree had proved less than easy. It had a ragged, broken look—

Then he understood why he was still alive. After being thrown from the saddle, he apparently had hit the tree. Its branches had bent under the impact, but its resiliency had bounced him to the side, onto his present spot on the ledge.

Rough as that treatment had been, it had saved him from falling at least another hundred feet. Whether such a reprieve might prove a mercy or a more cruel hoax, he was not at all certain.

Moving experimentally, he could find no broken bones, but such luck was a matter of degree. More than once, in cow camps, he had assisted the cook, pounding a tough beefsteak to a point where, after cooking, it was at least chewable. His body felt like the steak, after its working-over.

The diversity of pains seemed to have

consolidated, to have settled into one encompassing, solid ache. The warm beat of the sun, reflected back from the cliff side and rock on which he lay, scarcely eased the stiffness and soreness, but it was aggravating a raging thirst.

His mind was ready to accept this, knowing that injury or sickness brought an increased craving for water. But instinct did not accept so tamely that it must be inevitable. It stirred him to do something, however hard. But what?

To climb was out of the question. Reason and experience warned him that the shelf on which he lay was unlikely to lead anywhere, but at least there was a possibility. He could see it for half a hundred feet in either direction, before it seemed to turn or pinch out.

He was in no condition to walk, and even crawling was a slow task, which meant inching, dragging himself. His confusion made a mountain out of deciding which way he should go, but he decided that one way was as good as the other.

A hawk hung like a speck against the blue. Nothing else moved. Such breeze as roamed the heights was shut away by the walls, leaving only the concentrated heat of the sun.

Motion shocked fresh pain into being. Gasping, he lay while it subsided, then tried again, taking frequent pauses to rest. Time held no meaning.

He had reached something, but he had a sick sense he was being cheated. Without realizing, he had rounded the bend, but this was the end of the shelf—a dead end to the trail. It narrowed and pinched out, the wall above as sheer as ever, the drop at the side even less inviting.

Even the hawk had disappeared when he looked up. He was alone in an empty world.

Exactly when he turned and started back was hazy in his mind, but there was dry blood on the rock, and it roused him to realization. This was where he had lain during the hours of unconsciousness. He had made it back to his starting point.

To keep trying seemed futile, a hopeless effort, but thirst and the will to live combined to keep him at it. He reached the other turn, knowing a dragged-out moment of eagerness until he could see what lay beyond. Despair was like a kick in the face. It too, ended in a blank wall, just a few feet farther along.

He was trapped on the ledge, with nowhere to go.

He roused from a stupor, and realized that he had been crying, sobbing like a small boy, lost and fearful. There was no sense of shame, only a vast weariness.

But the sun had moved, and there was a small patch of shade which brought partial relief. The pain had eased, or grown more bearable. For the first time, he was able to think coherently, to fix his mind on something other than himself.

But, remembering what he had overheard the night before, he found that hardly an improvement. At the time, he had been too enraged against both Tiller-Parsons and Spotted Pony to think beyond the immediate aspects. The solution, it had seemed, was to deal with the chief. Had he succeeded, the problem would have been at least partly solved.

But he had failed, and now the vengeance-hungry chief would go on with his plan, attacking and killing. As with a weasel, the taste of blood would merely whet his appetite.

And the time, arranged between the two of them, was tonight!

The attack was planned as a total surprise, with no warning. He might have carried such a warning, had he used better judgment.

Forewarned, the ranch crew, implemented by the visitors, would still be heavily outnumbered, but they could at least put up a good fight. They deserved that much of a chance.

Even then, the outcome would be almost a certainty. Cut off from help, or any chance at escape, the odds would be too great, especially with a traitor in their midst!

But if he lacked any warning, the massacre would be as swift as it was ruthless.

He would be no better off, even if he could escape from this ledge and get word back, and neither would the others. Still, Montana Abbott was a soldier, with a reputation for leading hopeless causes. Given the chance, he might come up with a workable plan.

But the ability to think again was only another sort of torment. Even if uninjured, there was no chance either to climb or descend. The wall was too sheer, too tall. Though not as high here as back where he had lain, it was still a score of feet to the top.

Montana found sign pretty much where he had expected. Given the fact of Cassidy's absence, along with his being seen with

Tiller-Parsons prior to his disappearance—which Tiller-Parsons had strangely seen fit to deny—the answer was so sharply narrowed that little guesswork was involved.

There was nowhere else to go, no one else to send a message to, aside from Spotted Pony.

What such a message portended was chilling to think about. Yet again, considering all the circumstances, the humiliation which Tiller-Parsons had suffered, the answer was only too easy to guess.

The surface friendliness which prevailed at the moment between all the factions at the ranch, the careful courtesy on both sides, was after all no more than a veneer—especially with Tiller-Parsons under attack from many points.

He had been more than eager to call a truce, to extend every courtesy to their guests, who were also his employers. But once the Englishmen's visit was over and they were ready to start back, changes would be made. At the least, Tiller-Parsons would be out of a job. Almost as surely, he would be taken East to stand trial for bigamy, and very possibly other crimes. His career, which had promised so much, would be finished.

You judged a race horse on its past performances, a fighter on his record. On that basis, Tiller-Parsons' reaction was completely predictable. For him it had suddenly become a matter of all or nothing. With much less involved, he had betrayed women, used men as pawns, and not boggled at murder as a weapon.

That women were again involved could hardly be expected to deter him. His record showed him to be a monster. However jauntily he wore the cloak of respectability, tailored garments instead of buckskin, such clothes did not change the man.

Even without the confirmation which Cassidy might be able to give, Montana could pretty well envision what was in the wind, like a winter storm blowing down from the arctic. Having found sign, where Cassidy had come, he'd risk a little more in the hope of finding Cassidy. There seemed little doubt that Cassidy had stumbled into trouble.

If he had carried a message to Spotted Pony, the meeting place would more than likely be in that vicinity. Under the sun of high noon, the land looked peaceful, empty. But the sign was here, the trail made by a single horseman, spoor less than a day old.

That other eyes might be watching was so likely a possibility that his skin prickled. Now it had become like reading the pages of a book. One more turn of page or trail could bring a climax.

Here a second horseman had entered the picture. His pony had been unshod, so in all possibility it was an Indian cayuse. At this point its run had been suddenly checked; it had pivoted sharply, dancing impatiently while its rider took stock, before going on.

Back-tracking, Montana found a spatter of red, splashed like raindrops across the grass. There the trail ended, but the sudden deep gorge at one side was an explanation. Horse and rider had gone off together. Cassidy had acted, or perhaps reacted. His failure to return was easy to understand.

XVIII

The voice roused Cassidy from his stupor. It was persistent, insistent, disturbing. At first it seemed to be part of a dream which was more like a nightmare. Then, opening his eyes, he placed the sound. Montana was kneeling on the rim above, looking down, calling his name.

"Dutch!" he said urgently, as the latter stirred. "I'll lower a rope, Dutch. Get the noose over your head and under your arms, and I'll soon have you up here."

The end of a lariat plopped beside Cassidy's hand. Mechanically, Cassidy tried to obey, but the effort was too great. The last reserves of energy had been drained from him in crawling this far along the rocky shelf. His hand seemed to make a gesture of weary negation.

Montana was disappointed, but not very surprised. That a man could have gone off the trail and survived, even though caught on the ledge below, was more than he had expected. Now the impact of the fall, added to the long exposure, was taking its toll.

Had Cassidy been able to help himself, even to grasping the rope, it would have saved time and rendered his task immeasurably simpler. Since he could not, Montana considered the alternative. There was nothing, here at the top of the ledge, to which he might tie an end of the lariat, anchoring it while descending to Cassidy. The nearest object was a tree, half a hundred feet farther back, hopelessly out of reach.

There was just one chance, which he disliked. But it was either that, or ride away and leave Cassidy. If he did that, the injured man would be dead before he could return with help. He was clearly at the last extremity.

Even if he could hold out, there was not that much time to waste. The unfolding story was so clear as to be unmistakable. Like the storm, trouble was on the way. For whatever he might be worth, they would need him back at the ranch.

Montana chanced it, taking such insurance as was possible. A well-trained horse would stand groundhitched with the bridle reins dropped. But at the brink of a canyon, and under circumstances such as faced them, that would be expecting too much, even of a dependable animal. Never having ridden this horse before, he could not judge it. And the lives of both of them, his own as well as Cassidy's, depended on the result.

He found a good-sized stone not far back along the trail, lugged it, then tied the reins to it. Terror, a snorting plunge, could send the cayuse hurtling back, or cause the stone to slide over the brink. Either alternative might spoil the situation past retrieving. Yet it was the best he could do.

With the rope tied to the saddle-horn, Montana slid down it, onto the ledge beside Cassidy. Cassidy lay with eyes closed, his breathing so faint that Montana was not sure if he still lived. He unscrewed his canteen, placing it at Cassidy's lips. Water dribbled into his mouth, and after a moment, Cassidy choked, then roused to drink thirstily. His eyes opened on a note of wonder.

" 'Tis nectar from heaven," he breathed. "I didn't know till now that you wore wings—Montana."

"Let's get you out of this," Montana returned practically. "The sooner the better."

Somewhat revived by the water, Cassidy surveyed the rope, seeing the outline of the horse at the top of the cliff. His head shake was short but positive.

"A waste of time," he breathed. "I'm finished. And belike neither of us would make it."

"I can't leave you here."

"A dead man rests as easy one place as another. And I won't be keeping you long. Another sip of the water."

He drank again, then spoke urgently, though his voice was weakening, so that Montana had to bend close to hear.

"Tiller-Parsons sent me with a message to

Spotted Pony. Then they met, and I heard what they said. The Indians plan a massacre at the height of the—"

His voice ended in a sigh. Montana's breath echoed it. The need for helping him up from here was past. As he had said, one resting place was as good as another.

The pony shied and tried to pull back as Montana ascended, but with nothing to hinder him, he retained control. Had he been carrying an inert burden and trying to climb, it might have been a ticklish business.

Cassidy's meaning was clear. Montana had heard that one of the girls had suggested a ball, but apparently the same thought had already been in Tiller-Parsons' mind. His purpose, then, was to use the dance as a diversion. It would keep everyone occupied, and by the end of a long night they would be worn out, and then the attack would come.

From the point of view of the Indian, that was merely good generalship. But that a man of another race would lend himself to such duplicity, destroy his own people, was all but unbelievable.

At least, it would have been with most

men. In this case, Cassidy had heard the plot.

Montana pondered as he headed back. Foreknowledge should help, so that Dutch Cassidy's death might not be in vain. Even so, the prospects were bleak.

There were two alternatives. They could load up and set out at once, heading for the nearest settlement. Where days or weeks would be required, they would have only hours. If they were overtaken and surrounded, the chance for survival would be far less than within the shelter of the stout walls of the ranch house.

In it, they could stand off attacks for a while, since Spotted Pony would be denied the vital element of surprise. From there, they could make things more costly for the renegade band of braves.

But only for a while. Cut off from retreat, with no help possible and winter on the way, at best it would be only a matter of time.

Montana had more than once led forlorn causes, so finding himself in such a situation was nothing new. But to hit upon a plan, a scheme which offered a fighting chance for survival, was not easy. Between them, Spotted Pony and Tiller-Parsons had planned well.

The dance, or ball, was scheduled for that evening, so the attack would probably come at dawn. Ready, they could probably repel it, but that would be the beginning of a siege which they could have no hope of outlasting.

Even if a messenger could get out, there was nowhere to go for help; none that could or would be sent.

The attack was intended to come as a surprise, so if they were to have a chance, it had to be turned into a counter-surprise. Everything would hinge on that. Otherwise, the odds against them would lengthen with each hour, and the end would be as inevitable as it would be hopeless.

The alternative would hardly bear thinking about. Death in battle was one thing, and bad enough at best. But an Indian massacre was another matter entirely. With Spotted Pony cherishing an implacable hatred, his warriors would be ruthless. Survival, for any who escaped the initial assault, would be even worse.

He rode mechanically, leaving it to his horse to pick its own trail. Its sudden floundering plunge caught him by surprise. It was instinct, a natural reaction of muscles as well as mind, which enabled him to jump clear as the cayuse went down.

The pony was struggling to its feet again almost as quickly, eyes rolling in pain and terror. Montana needed only a glance to see what had happened, the cause as well as the effect. A front hoof had broken through and into a gopher hole, catching the limb, throwing the horse heavily. One look at the hanging leg, as the pony favored it, standing on three limbs, confirmed the bad news. The leg was broken.

There was nothing to do but to put the horse out of its misery, then plod on foot for the remaining distance. An already bad situation was compounded. For a while he was apprehensive that the gunshot might have been heard and would be investigated, but nothing happened. Even so, the delay was bad.

Darkness was falling when he came in sight of the ranch buildings. Tonight there would be a heavy darkness, for the long-threatening storm was beginning to move in, and clouds were obscuring the stars. But that was perhaps a small break in their favor.

Indians were as complex in nature as white

men, a prey to superstitions and fears in about equal degrees; it was mostly in type or character that their apprehensions differed. They liked to prowl by night, though at times they feared the dark, particularly in those hours just short of dawn. Having experienced those same hours many times, when sleep and the low bodily ebb slowed and confused the senses, Montana had no difficulty understanding such inhibitions.

Had the moon been riding high, they might have come loping in for an early attack, ranging like wolves. But in heavy, cloud-hung blackness, they would prefer to await the dawn, to strike as sleep followed exhaustion. It was a brief reprieve.

Lights were springing up all through the house, some with colored shades, the result of the decorators' ingenuity, lending a fairyland effect when viewed from a distance. Near the barn he made out extra wagons and buggies, showing that the invited guests from other ranches had arrived.

In the long run, with the raiders sweeping the country like a scythe, it might make little difference; but to receive special invitations to come to their deaths was as chilling as it was grim. It was a yardstick of the man who spun his web as a spider does.

An air of excitement, tinged with gaiety, could almost be felt. They were making a special effort to put all unpleasantness into the background, at least for the night. This party was in the nature of a housewarming, and they were determined to behave like civilized beings. With the exception of Tim O'Donnell, none suspected that peril might threaten.

As a tough ex-sergeant, O'Donnell would remain tight-lipped for as long as he dared. No one knew better the devastating effects of panic, so he would do his worrying in silence.

A shadowy figure was advancing to meet him. O'Donnell had been watching, his anxiety mounting as time dragged. Relief and apprehension mingled in his voice.

"Ah, Captain, it's happy I am to see you! I was beginning—" He broke off, suddenly realizing that Montana was on foot. "You've had difficulties?"

"Some. My horse put his foot in a gopher hole. I've had to walk."

O'Donnell expelled his breath in relief that it had been no worse. But Montana was alone.

"Cassidy—?"

"I found him dying. It seems he dueled

with Spotted Pony last night. He intended to stop the Indian, but it worked the other way. He was able to tell me what had happened—and what they plan."

O'Donnell had heard enough already to guess at the rest. The manner in which verbs and pronouns were linked was starkly revealing.

"I take it that Spotted Pony thinks his hour has come?"

"His plan is to wipe us out—probably at daylight."

"I had thought it was the storm I felt in my bones. The unholy devils!"

Knowing his meaning, Montana nodded. "Tiller-Parsons made the arrangements with Spotted Pony. Where is he?"

"Inside." O'Donnell's voice took on a quality of eagerness. "Let's go find him!"

XIX

The transformation had a quality of magic. The warmth of human companionship, the ingenuity of the workers, all combined against the background of loneliness to bring a lump to the throat, a mist before even the eyes of Henry Tiller-Parsons. Looking about, he knew a moment of doubt, a sense of regret. This was the sort of thing he had aimed for from the beginning, the kind of company he had hoped to attain. Ivory shoulders flashed above evening gowns, and laughter rippled like music.

His imagination was too active for his own enjoyment. He could think only of a flower garden in bloom, a field at harvest time—and the sudden total devastation of hail striking without warning, of red death at dawn—

It was worse than foolish to feel regret, particularly since the matter was now beyond his control. He had taken the realistic course, the only way possible. But it really was too bad.

A door opened, and he swung, starting at sight of Montana. O'Donnell was a step behind as they halted, gazing around. They were looking for somebody, and instinct assured Tiller-Parsons that he was the man. He had taken note of Abbott's absence, and as it grew prolonged, had decided that Montana would not be returning. He had ridden to look for Cassidy, and he had probably encountered some of Spotted Pony's band.

Panic replaced his sense of mild regret. Whatever Montana wanted, it would not be to his liking. There was no telling what Montana might have discovered, or at least been led to suspect.

Crowded as the big room was, they had not yet located him. Tiller-Parsons slipped quickly through a door into an adjoining room, then on out into the night.

Looking back, he drew a long breath. He had not been seen, but it would be better to keep out of sight for a while. In any case, he needed the fresh air to clear his head—

A scream rose in his throat, choked short of utterance, as a shadowy figure leaped, knocking him backward. An elbow crooked about his neck as he sprawled; then bony knees were upon his chest, and a painted, savage face was leering above. A heavy, greasy stench, compounded of all those things which he found most distasteful, was in Tiller-Parsons' nostrils. Clutching fingers loosened from his throat to tangle in his hair. A long blade was lifted, poised. . . .

"He was here," O'Donnell said worriedly. "But he must have seen you first!"

"It doesn't really matter," Montana decided. "Our first job is to alert everybody to the danger, to be as ready as we can for the attack when it comes."

Since he had not been bothered on his way back, he doubted if Spotted Pony's warriors would be along, at least in force, until later in the night. But they might already be on the watch. A break in the tempo of the party might warn them and bring a speedy assault, before they could ready themselves for it.

"We'll mingle with the others and pass the word—one person at a time," Montana decided. "Make sure that everybody keeps on as though nothing were happening."

Montana noted with satisfaction but no particular surprise that the news was taken in stride. Cheeks paled, feet faltered in the dance, then regained their tempo. There was no panic, not even unnecessary questions. Montana gave his news first to Sir John and Mr. Gates.

"Please don't let on, gentlemen, but I have some unpleasant news," he said. "I believe you've heard of Chief Spotted Pony and his band—some renegade braves who have long been trouble-makers. They are getting ready to attack us. They may strike during the night, but probably will hit at about daylight. Should our actions betray to them that we suspect an attack, that might hurry them before we could ready a defense. Yet we must be prepared to defend ourselves at any moment."

Gates' calm did not desert him. Sir John looked thoughtfully at his half-emptied glass.

"I've rather had the feeling that something was amiss," he acknowledged. "Cave-man instinct, perhaps. You're taking charge?"

"Unless you have other preferences," Montana agreed. "It's a nasty situation, but not hopeless."

"As bad as that, eh? Well, carry on. We're with you."

O'Donnell explained to Rose. Her eyes grew large as she listened, but she confirmed the opinion he had already formed. In the face of trouble, she would be as steady as any man.

"It's going to be bad, isn't it?" she asked.

O'Donnell was grimly honest.

"Without Montana to handle things, it would be. But he has a reputation for doing the impossible. Tell the other women—but don't let on that anything is amiss. I'll be passing out guns."

Rose seemed to take reassurance from what she saw in his face.

"Of course. And I have confidence in you

as well. So, Timothy—should the worst happen—"

O'Donnell's eyes betrayed his anguish, but his nod was casual.

"In such an eventuality, I will save a couple of bullets," he promised. "Be sure of that, girl."

The house was a strange contradiction, in some aspects approaching a mansion, in others as primitive as its surroundings. The walls were mostly of logs, solid enough to stop bullets or turn arrows, but the doors were flimsy, and there were no loopholes for rifles, which would have seemed an obvious precaution. Many of the windows were covered with oiled deerhide, scraped thin, the frontier's substitute for glass. These had no shutters.

A few of the windows were glass, and with the interior brilliantly lighted, their movements could be watched from the outer darkness; since a sudden volley could take them by surprise, they covered those windows on the inside with blankets. But at best it would be a flimsy shelter in which to withstand attack.

Something with which to counter the attack, in addition to guns, was imperative. But a more thorough ransacking of the supplies was discouraging. Montana had hoped that an ample supply of powder might have been included with the most recent arrival, but there was none. Whether this oversight was deliberate or due merely to carelessness on the part of Tiller-Parsons, the effect was the same.

A considerable excess of small hardware, nails, nuts and bolts, remained from the carpenters' supplies. These, mixed in buckets of powder, could be used to make bombs which, exploded by gunfire, would be devastating in their effect. A score, or only a dozen, buried at ground level and strategically scattered outside, might reverse the odds when the warriors came crowding.

That was what Montana had hoped for. Instead, finding barely enough powder for a single bomb, he eyed it in dismay. Incongruously enough, there was a handful of caps to insure an explosion when a bullet struck, but so heavy and clumsy a bucketful could hardly be tossed out with much chance of proving effective. Concealed in advance, the odds of it being in the right place at the right time were a hundred to one.

Should it prove a dud, their enemies would only be further enraged that nothing remained to use against them.

Coming to stand beside Montana, O'Donnell shook his head. As a former sergeant, he understood what Montana had intended and how paltry a single bomb could be. From an adjoining room, the wail of a fiddle and the scrape of boots lent a further note of mockery.

"I'd had the same notion, Cap'n," he observed dejectedly. "This could be a help—used when and where needed. But once they start, they'll do the picking, not us."

"Maybe," Montana conceded. "On the other hand—" he was thinking aloud—"Spotted Pony was educated in the white man's ways. He hates them, but still they influence him. There just might be a chance—"

He picked up the laden bucket, then a shovel in his other hand.

"The fix we're in, we make the most of any sort of a chance. Pull that long face into something a little less discouraged and go dance with the ladies—all of them. I've a trap to set."

He slipped out into the night, quickly moving away from the door. For a long moment he stood as patiently as a cat, ears and eyes strained, testing the dark. Nothing moved, and the only sounds came from inside the house.

Choosing a spot at some distance, he dug, easing the shovel in and out of the soil as though the bomb were already in place and might be set off at a touch. The night held an eerie quality. The clash of steel against a stone might bring an attack.

When a small pit was excavated, he lowered the pail into it, then replaced the dirt around it, so that the ground remained level. A torn piece of sacking, thrown carelessly, concealed the operation.

The essence of setting a trap was either to hide it completely, or to leave sign so obvious that it would not be associated with a trap.

Candlelight and soft music contrasted strangely with rifles and revolvers, placed handily, the barrels reflecting back the light. Every man, including the English, wore a cartridge belt and holstered revolver, and was accordingly hampered in the more intricate movements of the dance. Beyond these preparations, they made a courageous pretense that there was nothing unusual about the night.

One of the visiting ranchers had suggested the possibility of posting men in the barn and other outbuildings, but Montana had vetoed that. Their forces were too small to be scattered, then cut off. It had to be the house or nothing.

Whether the enemy were already outside, or in those buildings, they could only speculate. Montana's guess was that, aside from a few scouts who would keep watch, Spotted Pony would hold his warriors well back until the time for attack. In any event, they gave no sign.

Neither did his own party, who gallantly maintained the pretense of enjoying themselves. If cheeks appeared paler under the candlelight, voices remained steady, the glances from feminine eyes challenging as well as sparkling. There was nothing to do but wait out the night. The initiative rested with Spotted Pony.

Tiller-Parsons had not returned. His continued absence went unremarked but not unnoticed.

That the enemy was almost certainly close at hand, yet waiting out the night, stretched nerves almost to the breaking point. But Spotted Pony, in addition to following custom, knew the value of patience. If their victims had been forewarned and were expecting an attack, the strain was in his favor. Should the attack come as the surprise which it was intended to be, weariness and a general let-down would follow so long a night. Dawn would be the hour.

Even the pretense ran heavily as a faint grayness became visible at the edges of the blankets. Montana gave them credit; a disciplined regiment could have done no better. Bravery was not a lack of fear; it was holding steady when apprehension choked like dust in the mouth, poured with the heaviness of lead in the veins.

Daylight was slow in coming, held back by a heavy pall of cloud. To anyone inclined to give way to superstition, the omens were unchancy. But that could apply equally well to the other side.

Attack came, predictably, with a sudden wild screeching, punctuated by the blasting of guns, of arrows making sudden tears in the taut deerskins. A pane of glass shattered. But everyone was prompt to take a pre-assigned position, making use of the scanty light to pick targets and return a devastating fire.

A war axe slit the hide at a window, warriors piling through. Their own eager rush choked them, and axes at direct range, in addition to guns, cleared the space as suddenly. The surging wave of men hesitated, broke and drew back. One of the visiting ranchers was jubilant.

"They got more'n they bargained for," he observed. "And it'll be raining pretty soon, a real storm from the look of things. That's all to the good, for us."

Montana did not delude himself. They could probably hold, but a siege would go against them. If they were to survive, this must be decided quickly. By now, it was almost light enough to make his move.

A second wave of warriors swept at them, but by now the light was against them. The interior of the house would soon become a shambles, but its walls afforded good shelter from which to pick and choose when firing. Even frenzied enthusiasm could not stand so raking a fire, while there were no targets in return.

Again they pulled back. This would be his chance, if there was any hope. Opening a door a crack, Montana thrust a white flag ahead.

The neighboring rancher scowled. "What's the idea?" he demanded. "You ain't aimin' to surrender?"

"Just to parley, if they will," Montana explained. "Spotted Pony knows the meaning of such a signal. Let's hope he'll respond."

Among the milling warriors, there was hesitation. Then, in a gesture which emphasized his contempt, Spotted Pony stepped into the open. It was a gesture of courage if not of trust.

Montana opened the door wide in turn. "Are you willing to parley, Spotted Pony?"

The chief shrugged. "*We* have nothing to lose," he said.

XX

Even the scream in Tiller-Parsons' throat seemed, like the hand on his neck, to be strangling him. Above him, shadowy but savage, a merciless face wavered, the eyes glaring like those of a cat. Tiller-Parsons could do no more than thresh wildly with feet and legs.

Then a voice grunted sharply, a powerful hand plucked his antagonist from him, and the chief was looking from one to the other with his usual mixture of disgusted contempt. Tiller-Parsons swallowed painfully, sucking in a gasping breath.

"Thanks, Chief," he stammered. "I was

coming to find you. Your man made a mistake."

Spotted Pony did not deign to ask what he wanted or what sort of a message he might bring. Tonight, he was the unbendingly hostile savage who had seized him several days before, on the way to the ranch. That time, Tiller-Parsons had been able to talk him out of it, but on that occasion he had had something to offer. Now Spotted Pony was in control, and he enjoyed showing his contempt.

"No mistake," he grunted. "You fool—all white men fools." He gave an order in his own tongue, the words unintelligible to Tiller-Parsons. Obeying, ignoring the white man's struggles and protests, the warrior who had been on the point of scalping him, assisted by another brave, hustled him to a small, remote shed. The full measure of their disregard was that they did not try to stop him from screaming or calling out, but he remained silent from very hopelessness.

The closing door was the beginning of a long night. The shed was windowless, the darkness almost total. Two truths became apparent to Tiller-Parsons as the hours wore on and he was left alone. The first was the implacable nature of the man he had thought to use, the unrelenting hatred of Spotted Pony for all whites. And his own conduct, he realized belatedly, had only served to reinforce the contempt and rage.

He was being left alive, at least for a while, but despite the blackness he saw clearly for the first time. Holding him so was only another measure of the Indian's contempt, an additional expression of hate. Knowing what was to come at daylight, they were hours of torment. Tiller-Parsons had no slightest doubt that he was slated to die with the rest.

Exhaustion overcame him, and he slept fitfully. When he finally roused and fumbled uncertainly at the door, he was bewildered to find that it had not been locked.

Perhaps it was his training among the whites. Spotted Pony stood an instant, his stare baleful. Then he gestured.

"Wait," he said, and moved to the corner of the barn. Montana heard his order; then another man appeared, leading a pony. Spotted Pony placed his hands on its back and vaulted lightly to a seat. He rode out, controlling the cayuse with voice and knees. From that vantage point he was able to look down.

There was a touch of the majestic in the

gesture. He halted midway between the house and barn, and this was what Montana had expected. His warriors remained near the barn, restrained, but as eager as hounds in sight of their prey.

Spotted Pony gestured, expressing jointly an invitation and a command. It was up to Montana, if he wished to parley, to come to him.

O'Donnell spoke softly.

"I'll be holdin' a bead on that oily devil—but they figure they have us for sure."

The faint jingle of Montana's spurs was the only sound as he crossed the open. Apparently no one noticed, or thought to wonder about that. He had removed the spurs the evening before, before dancing with anyone. Already, the warmth and forced gaiety of the ball seemed remote, to belong to the long ago.

It had been an interlude, at once pleasant and frightening. He had held each of the women in his arms, Rose, Alicia, Jennifer—lips which laughed, even while their eyes could not quite hide the terror of the day now dawning. The memory held his footsteps steady. Even so, and short as it was, those paces were by way of being the longest walk he had ever taken. It was like the final steps to the gallows.

This was the showdown, with everything on the board. Life or death, and not merely his own, must hinge on the turn of a single card. The certainty that he held all the high cards was the only reason Spotted Pony even made a pretense at a parley.

Spotted Pony controlled his impatient horse easily, his will seeming to communicate itself to the cayuse. His warriors held steady, but they were as twitchingly eager as a cat poised to pounce. Montana ignored them.

"Well?" Spotted Pony flung the word as a challenge. He could not forbear a taunt. "Talk—dead man."

The initial steps had been an ordeal. It was always so, like a plunge into icy water. Once a man was immersed, the shock was forgotten. Hands loose at his sides, Montana halted. His holstered revolver was in easy reaching distance, but Spotted Pony was contemptuously certain that he would grab for it only as a last desperate resort.

"Dead *men* talk," Abbott corrected. "You and I. Don't make any mistake, Chief. If I die, you'll embark on that journey right along with me. Are you in a hurry to reach those new hunting gounds?"

Spotted Pony was not impressed. He understood the brag and bluff of white men.

"Listen to the wind!" he mocked. "But we do not crouch in the tepee before the storm! We *are* the blizzard!"

Montana took a backward, faltering step. Every mocking eye was on his face rather than his feet. Nobody noticed as the rowel of his spur hooked the sacking and dragged it back. Since the bucket it had uncovered was on a level with the surrounding surface, it attracted no attention.

Montana gave an impatient shake of his foot, but the ragged piece of cloth still clung. He tried again, then bent and tore it loose. It was a small byplay, which seemed to express his humiliation and uncertainty. It was as he straightened that they saw the gun in his hand, clear of the holster. For the moment, it threatened no one.

"A winter storm blows cold," Montana agreed. "Its arrows are tipped with death! Shall the coyotes feast?"

Spotted Pony hated himself for being impressed. The gun in hand was like the magic of a medicine man, and it confirmed the reports he'd heard of Montana, tales which he had contemptuously dismissed. His grunt echoed his doubt.

"White man brag! White man lie!" The sound of his voice fanned his fury. "White man die!"

The clouds had drawn in from every point of the compass, their grayness delaying the full coming of daylight. A feel of storm was in the air. Spotted Pony had spoken of the blizzard, and Montana had no doubt that one was on the way. This dawn held all the portents of trouble.

A hush followed the chief's bluster. Somehow, even in his own ears, his words were empty. Then a crow appeared, just over their heads and flying low, as though fleeing the storm.

Montana took a chance. Any move might trigger an onslaught, but this was all part of a calculated gamble. As before, the onlookers failed to see the motion of the gun, but they heard the shot. Then the crow was thudding almost at the feet of the chief, a spatter of dark feathers hanging poised in the air above, then fluttering around him. A collective gasp of dismay went up from the watching braves at so ill an omen.

"That shot was just to show you," Montana informed him, and now the talk was straight. "I could have killed you. If I shoot again, it will be at that keg of powder." His eyes indicated the bucket to the startled watchers. "If I have to shoot instead of parley, we both die—and not us alone, Chief. You know what powder can do. A pinch of it is death." The dead crow no longer fluttered, but the gun was a poised threat. Spotted Pony's eyes studied the bucket. It was trickery, and he had long held white men in contempt for trickery, even while envying them their ability. He did not doubt the threat. Whatever might be said of this particular white man, even his enemies admitted that he did not speak with a forked tongue.

He had consented to parley because of his certainty that he was in complete control of the situation. Now he hesitated. Triumph was like dust on his tongue. To back down, even to save his life, was unthinkable. He was Spotted Pony, and not as other men.

For Spotted Pony was a renegade, even in the eyes of most of his tribe. He had disdained the council fires, riding wide, leading his lawless group, boasting of his hate and what he was going to do.

Better now to die than to back down, to

live a legend than to die at long last in shame. And yet—

Uncertainty gnawed, like a rat at a wheat stalk. His shamed glance strayed; then his eyes widened at sight of the man who was advancing, moving like a sleepwalker. Fury surged up from Spotted Pony's throat, stinging like heartburn. Even Tiller-Parsons was in on this, having lured him to a trap—

Wild fury erupted from his throat in a gobbling shriek. He drove his pony at Abbott, snatching for his tomahawk as the cayuse jumped.

He was calling the bluff, but Montana had not been bluffing. As the gun muzzle swung, the chamber was emptying in a roaring fusillade, lost and swallowed in the overwhelming thunder of the blast.

XXI

To lift first one arm and then the other, coming upright as slowly and awkwardly as a half-frozen cow, was mechanical, an instinctive reaction. The blast itself had subsided, but its roaring still pounded in his head. Montana looked about dazedly, his mind as fuzzy as the flakes of snow which were drifting from the leaden sky.

He was torn and bloody, but alive. The latter was the astonishing part, for he'd had no expectation of surviving at such close range to the blast. Then he understood that the confusion was not all in his mind. There was moaning and yelping, on a subdued and frantic note, with scant resemblance to the gobble of the war whoop. Then came the diminishing pounding of hoofs.

The buildings were intact, but a gaping crater yawned where he had sunk the bucket of powder. Dirt and debris filled the open spaces, even the nearer roofs.

Further movement disclosed no broken bones, despite burns and bruises. The blood was on the outside, and not his own.

Tim O'Donnell was the first to reach him, though others were close behind. The ex-sergeant set an arm about Montana's shoulders as he staggered.

"Glory be, you're alive!" he breathed. "Which I'd never have bet good money on!"

"I guess I am," Montana admitted, but his mind still boggled at the results.

"The chief was right on top of that charge of powder when it went off," O'Donnell said soberly. "He was trying to come at you, though it seemed to be the sight of Tiller-Parsons that set him crazy. His horse took the full force of the blast, and sort of smothered or contained it, I guess. On that account, it didn't do nearly the damage that it might have. It killed a couple of the Indians, along with Tiller-Parsons, and scared the daylights out of the rest of them. I reckon they'll run till their horses drop."

Montana was beginning to understand. The result had been freakish, but even better than he had hoped. Though neither Tiller-Parsons nor Spotted Pony had intended it that way, they had played decisive roles.

O'Donnell summed it up sardonically.

"To give credit where it's due, I guess we could say that pair went out in a blaze of glory!"

The storm had dumped a couple of feet of snow, but it had been no blizzard. The white blanket had covered all signs of strife, as though in promise of a new era.

"Sure and I'm as lucky a man as you," O'Donnell confided jubilantly to Montana. "You are alive and in good shape, and I have won a woman like Rose! She's agreed to marry me—and this time it will *be* a marriage! Seems she likes this country, which is sort of surprising, everything considered."

"She found you here, didn't she?" Montana countered. "That works both ways, you know. I'd say you both deserve it."

Horatio Gates came up as O'Donnell moved away. He had been checking the books and papers left behind by Tiller-Parsons.

"It's rather too bad that the old boy got off on the wrong trail, then rode it so hard," he observed. "He had an amazing amount of talent. What he accomplished here is outstanding. Well, at least his luck didn't all desert him at the last. Considering all the circumstances, I can't think of a better ending to his problems."

"Will you all be staying for a big game hunt?" Montana asked.

"I think not. We were hoping for a bit of adventure, and that has been provided. They are all agreed that we'd best be heading back before the snows get too deep. I'm sure we'll all remember our stay here."

His tone became brisk.

"Another excellent choice on Tiller-Parsons' part—perhaps better than he intended—was to hire you, Montana. But you're not the sort who requires two or three men to do a job. So, in addition to being ranch foreman, I'm hoping that you will act as our manager over here as well. We're all agreed that you've done an excellent job."

Montana had foreseen the offer and had toyed with the idea of accepting it. But now—

"I appreciate your good opinion," he said. "But I guess I'm what is called fiddle-footed."

"You mean you will be moving on?"

Abbott nodded, watching where O'Donnell and Rose were laughing together. She would walk proudly beside her man under any circumstances, but a gentlewoman of her quality deserved something more than a sod hut or a homestead shack. This big house would be a fitting setting—

"Well, we're too deeply in your debt to try to persuade you against your will." Gates sighed. "But your decision leaves me with a problem. Men with the ability to manage an outfit such as this are not easy to come by. As one of the cowboys remarked, they don't exactly clutter up the landscape."

"But luck is where you find it," Montana suggested. "Why not offer the job to O'Donnell? Since he's to be married, he'll have need of a good job. And from what I have seen of him, I'm sure he'll handle it competently."

"An excellent suggestion." Horatio Gates was too much of a gentleman to betray his sudden insight into Montana's motives. But all at once he was forced to blow his nose with unnecessary loudness.

The publishers hope that this
Large Print Book has brought
you pleasurable reading.
Each title is designed to make
the text as easy to see as possible.
G.K. Hall Large Print Books
are available from your library and
your local bookstore. Or, you can
receive information by mail on
upcoming and current Large Print Books
and order directly from the publishers.
Just send your name and address to:

G.K. Hall & Co.
70 Lincoln Street
Boston, Mass. 02111

or call, toll-free:

1-800-343-2806

A note on the text
Large print edition designed by
Kipling West.
Composed in 16 pt Plantin
on a Xyvision 300/Linotron 202N
by Tara Casey
of G.K. Hall & Co.